A Tale of Christmas Present

A Time-Travel Novel

By Katelyn A. Brown

Dedication

*For my sister, Taressa. My best friend, trusted
confidante, super aunt, and faithful listener
—no one quite gets me like you do. Thanks for
always being there for me. I love you!*

Prologue

December 1883

Avery Cole signed her name in ink, leaving the paper to dry on the table for a moment. She pulled her shawl more tightly around herself and got up to stoke the fire, adding more wood and coaxing it to roaring blaze. Her fingers traced the children's handmade Christmas decorations strewn across the mantle. Icy wind howled across the prairie, but she was snug and warm inside.

Checking the paper and satisfied she wouldn't smudge the ink, Avery folded it and tiptoed up the stairs. The twins didn't always take an afternoon nap, but they had been tired today due to a nasty cold they were both fighting.

She quietly opened her door, praying the creaking wouldn't wake them, and opened the old trunk. Moving various items out of the way, her fingers found their way to the now-familiar secret compartment, and she placed the letter to her old friend inside.

December 15, 1883
Dear Aggie,

I'm sorry it's been a while since I last wrote you. Most days have been so busy I can scarcely think! The past year has brought many changes to our family. After the railroad was completed through town, the Orphan Train came through for the first time. Jake and I had been talking about taking in a child, but when we saw Lily and Matthew, we knew we couldn't split them up. They are three-year-old twins, whose parents died in an outbreak of scarlet fever in New York.

I won't say it's been an easy year...it's been a long road establishing trust, but I'm so glad they are a part of our family. Their little personalities are starting to shine through after so much sadness in their young lives.

Lizzie is shooting up like a weed and bossing everyone around, as usual. She's eleven now and asks me almost daily why she still has to go to school! Truthfully, she's a great help to me around the house and is wonderful at occupying the younger children, but you know how I feel about education.

Drew's latest scrape is a sprained ankle. He tripped and fell while racing Thomas and James Johnson. He's currently hobbling around the house with a makeshift cane Jake fashioned for him. Luckily, that boy will read anything he gets his hands on, so he's spending a lot of time with his foot elevated and his nose in a book. How I wish there was a library here! A few friends and I swap books sometimes, so the kids have new material, and lately Drew's taken to writing his own stories.

Caroline is wild as ever! She wants to grow up so

fast and keep up with the big kids, but there's still much of that rambunctious toddler in her that I first met. Becoming a big sister has been good for her and she loves to play with Lily and Matt when she comes home from school (I can't believe she's old enough for that!).

We're all looking forward to our first Christmas as a family of seven. The ranch is busy and Jake's hoping for a good sale after spring calving. He's wanting to purchase more land to expand the ranch.

How are things at the museum? Are you and your family well? I miss you so much!

Love,
Avery

November 7, 2016
My dearest Avery,

I hope this letter finds you well. It's been a while since I've had an update from you. How are Jacob and the kids? I hope the ranch expansion is gong smoothly for you all!

Things are good here, although it's been very busy. The shop next door went out of business last year, so I've been making plans. Next week, Aggie's Café and Antique Shop will officially open! It's been a fun project for me and will hopefully bring more traffic and revenue to our downtown area.

In other news, I've had another great-grandbaby born three months ago, and she's just the sweetest thing. I'm thankful she's close to give this old Granny lots of snuggles. Our whole crew will be descending on Redbud Grove in a few weeks for Thanksgiving—you know it's one of my favorite times!

Hope to hear from you soon.

Love,

Aggie

June 3, 1885

Dear Aggie,

Just hoping to scratch out a quick note while the baby's napping—my one quiet time of the day. The rest of the kids will be home from school soon, and chaos will reign once again. Oh, you read that right, I said baby! Hannah is almost a year old and came to live with us after she was the only survivor of a house fire the next town over. The doc knew of our troubles conceiving and asked if we could take her in. Of course, we said yes.

This is not the family I envisioned...but even with all our challenges, I wouldn't trade it for anything. We are so glad we were able to adopt Lily, Matt and now baby Hannah. I can't imagine life without them. Our family of eight feels complete. Everyone adores doting on Hannah and she's probably going to become quite spoiled...but we all can't seem to help it.

Jake is looking into hiring a ranch hand. I've not been able to help quite as much with Hannah's arrival, and his workload is ever-increasing! He says that's a good problem to have.

I hope this letter finds you well. I'm excited to hear all about how the café and shop are doing!

Love,

Avery

Chapter 1

"Even to your old age I am he, and to gray hairs I will carry you. I have made, and I will bear; I will carry and I will save...remember the former things of old; for I am God, and there is no other; I am God, and there is none like me, declaring the end from the beginning and from ancient times things not yet done, saying, 'My counsel shall stand, and I will accomplish all my purpose.'"
Isaiah 46:4,9-10

November 2018

The packing tape screeched as Jovie Campbell stretched it across the cardboard box full of bed linens. She added it to the growing stack along the wall of her bedroom.

"Are you sure about this?" Jovie's roommate, Maxine, appeared in the doorway with a fresh supply of boxes. "You know you can stay, and I'll help any way that I can."

"I know, Max...thanks. I have to do this, though. I need a change of scenery and a new start." Jovie glanced down at her expanding belly. Her jeans wouldn't button anymore, so she had opted for her most forgiving leggings and an oversized sweater.

"Can you at least wait until you have more of a plan?" Max asked.

"If I think about it too much, I might chicken out," Jovie replied.

"Exactly," Max shot back.

Jovie stood and hugged her friend. "I'm going to miss you," she said simply.

Maxine's eyes looked suspiciously wet. "Me, too."

Jovie never would have suspected even a couple of months ago that her life would have taken such a drastic turn, but life was full of surprises, and a lot had changed since then. The moment the line turned pink on the home pregnancy test, Jovie knew her life would never be the same.

When she'd met Parker at a work event months before, his charming and charismatic personality had drawn her in immediately. They'd casually dated, but it had really been more of a fling than anything serious for either of them. Until that night they'd gone out with his friends, and things had gotten out of hand.

Jovie didn't ordinarily drink much. One horrible hangover as a teenager had been enough for her to steer clear of the hard stuff. And even now, she cringed at the thought of what a cliché she'd become —a few too many cocktails to loosen up in front of new friends, and then finding herself pregnant a few weeks later. Her memory of the night was a blur, and she'd ended up staying the night at Parker's place. Neither of them was in any frame of mind to be bothered with protection.

Jovie thought back to her most recent conversation with Parker, and the look of shock and disbelief all over his face when she'd shared her news. They weren't together anymore, but she thought he had a right to know. However, he wasn't as supportive as she'd hoped. Oh, he'd offered her money—he had plenty of that. But he'd just accepted a new job in Dallas, and he really couldn't see himself being a father so soon. She'd driven away from his apartment in disgust, tears stinging her eyes and overcome by utter desperation at her predicament.

Jovie had always wanted to be a mother. She thought, perhaps, she might even be good at it. She just didn't think she'd be finding out so soon, not to mention going it alone. She really wasn't sure at all what she wanted to do about the pregnancy.

And then she'd gone to her first doctor's appointment. When she saw the tiny, jumping heartbeat on the fuzzy, black-and-white screen, she knew there was no going back. She wanted this child, more than she ever thought possible. Even if the baby was Parker's.

"I guess it'll just be you and me, kid," she'd whispered to her belly when the doctor left the room.

In the next few weeks, Jovie had battled extreme fatigue and nausea that came and went all day long. Nevertheless, she made some life-changing decisions. Perhaps she wasn't in the best frame of mind to do so, but she felt as though it were now or never.

She immediately began looking for a new job. When she had graduated college a little over three years before, it turned out that following her passion for history did not a job offer make. So, when she'd landed a random marketing gig with a large company, she was just happy to have a steady paycheck, despite the soul-sucking corporate environment. She had been saving ever since and had built up quite a nest egg. The income had also allowed her to finish her master's degree.

Jovie knew she wanted to get out of Kansas City. She needed a new start and wanted to put down roots in a smaller community. She had traveled all over during her own childhood. Even now, her parents were living abroad in Dubai and her brother had moved to California. Growing up all over the world had its own perks, but at the moment, her only desire was stability.

When Redbud Grove popped into her mind, Jovie immediately got on a real estate app and searched for rentals, soon followed by checking out job listings. Just a few hours from the city, Jovie had wonderful memories of visiting her Uncle Wayne and Aunt Darla's farm outside the quaint small town. Uncle Wayne was the opposite of his adventurous sister, Jovie's mother, in every way. He and Jovie shared a mutual fascination with history, and their family had owned the farmland where he and Darla lived for over a hundred years.

Jovie checked the job openings nearly every

day for two weeks, but there weren't many opportunities in the small town. She couldn't believe her luck when, one day, she stumbled onto a job listing for an emergency substitute history professor at the small university on the edge of town. Thanks to those online and night classes, Jovie was qualified to teach at the college level. She could hardly contain her excitement that she might finally get to work in her chosen field as she prepared her resume and filled out the application.

The university was eager to fill the spot quickly. After a phone interview and thanks to some great recommendations from her former professors, soon a job offer was on the table. She would be teaching American History, Geography, and History of Western Civilization, for the next calendar year. Jovie hoped it would get her foot in the door to something more permanent. She was happy to have a steady job, as well as good health insurance. The baby was due in May, so she hoped to make it through the spring semester before delivering.

Meanwhile, the real estate on the market in the small town moved sluggishly with few options. Finally, Jovie saw a new listing for a small apartment. *It's perfect,* she thought. The renovated, two-bedroom upstairs unit overlooked the town square. The next day, she forwarded the security deposit, signed her electronic signature on the lease, and began packing.

Maxine thought she was insane to move to a strange, small town, apartment and job sight-unseen. Maybe she was crazy. But despite the unknown, Jovie was eager to start this new chapter of her life.

∞∞∞

November 1890

Lizzie Cole urged the team of horses forward. She had been keen to go to town for the supplies Avery, her stepmother, needed. But darkness was fast approaching, and the temperature dropped steadily, making her long for the warm fires of home.

Lately, when she thought of the Kansas ranch on which she'd grown up, it still gave her a comforting feeling, but it was also accompanied by a restlessness she couldn't seem to shake. Lizzie was eighteen years old now, and eager spread her wings. She just didn't know exactly how to go about it. Her best friend, Grace, had already married and settled down with the town blacksmith's son, Harrison. Lizzie expected they would announce their growing family any day.

Most of her girlhood chums were pairing off and doing the same. She knew that's what was expected of her, but she didn't know if she could fit into that mold. Not to mention, she didn't fancy any of the young men she knew. The thought of marrying and starting a family so soon honestly felt rather stifling to Lizzie. She wanted to see the world and travel to new places.

She could become a teacher or a nurse, but neither profession really appealed to her. She had never been the best student, and the thought of blood and bodily fluids made her stomach turn. But what else was she to do?

Perhaps she should talk to Avery about the disconcerting thoughts swirling in her head. Her stepmother had rather modern thoughts about women and worked side-by-side with her father, Jacob, helping run the cattle ranch and farm.

Avery had come into their lives ten years before, and she and the Cole family had saved one another, both literally and figuratively. They were all a little broken and hurting from losing people they'd loved. Avery's arrival had been surrounded in mystery, seemingly just when they needed her, and she needed them. Even now, Lizzie didn't know much about her stepmother's life before she came to live with them. Avery rarely spoke of it.

Just a few weeks after becoming their housekeeper and nanny, Avery saved Lizzie's little sister, Caroline, when she nearly fell through some thin ice just before her third birthday. Lizzie still shuddered at the images burned into her memory—Avery plunging into the icy pond waters instead of Caroline, her father pulling her out, and the hours of agony waiting to learn that she would be okay. Avery had become an integral part of Lizzie's family ever since that fateful day.

Passing a copse of trees and rounding a bend in the worn wagon road, the Cole ranch came into view. Lizzie urged the horses the last few yards to the barn. Thankfully, her brother Drew and their hired hand,

Noah, were there. They offered to unhitch and stable the horses for her. Saying her thanks, Lizzie loaded up her parcels and hurried to the tall white house, the windows already aglow with the lantern light inside.

As usual, the Cole home was a busy hive of activity. Lizzie dropped the parcels on the table. Avery gave her a quick hug of thanks, while four-year-old Hannah launched herself into Lizzie's legs.

"Oof!" Lizzie said, trying to undo her wraps and detangle Hannah from her body. Caroline chopped vegetables in the kitchen while Lily and Matt thundered up the stairs, sounding as if they would fall clean through the ceiling any minute.

"Come sit with me by the fire while I warm up," Lizzie said, hanging up her things and scooping Hannah into her arms. They sat in the rocker together before the roaring fire, and all was peaceful for a few moments while Hannah snuggled into Lizzie. But the little girl soon began to squirm and wanted to show Lizzie her doll's tea party, so Lizzie let herself be led up the stairs to the girls' room.

Chapter 2

November 2018

T he front door of the farmhouse flew open as
Aunt Darla rushed down the steps toward Jovie's car. Jovie stepped out, stretching out the
kinks from driving the last few hours. Uncle Wayne
waved from his porch rocker, grinning, as Darla threw
her arms around her favorite, and only, niece. When
Darla pulled back, she glanced down at Jovie's belly,
resting her hands lightly on the small bump that
couldn't be hidden on her thin, willowy frame. She
raised her eyes to Jovie's, confusion written in them.

"Oh, honey, why didn't tell us?" Darla asked.

"I wasn't sure what to say," Jovie shrugged. She
had come to terms with what was happening, and her
friends had been supportive, but it had been more
difficult to tell her family. She had only video chatted
with her parents a couple weeks ago, finally inform-
ing them of the pregnancy and her plans to move.
They had raised her to be independent, but she could
see they were concerned about her future. The news
that she would be living near her aunt and uncle had

seemed to appease them.

Jovie's aunt wrapped a comforting arm around her shoulder and led her to the house. Before she knew it, she was in Wayne and Darla's kitchen, sipping hot tea with honey and spilling the whole story. Wayne's solid hand patted her shoulder while Darla voiced her disapproval at Parker's reaction.

"Why don't you stay with us for a while, Jo?" Darla asked, reverting to Jovie's childhood nickname.

Jovie shook her head. She was grateful for their support, but she wanted to stand on her own two feet. "No, I've already signed my contract for the place in town. It will be good to be so close to the university, and I'm really looking forward to making it my own. But, thank you. I'm glad to know you'll be nearby."

Uncle Wayne glanced at her car out the window, piled to the brim with boxes. "We'll come with you to unload all your stuff and get you settled. But where's all your furniture?"

"The apartment is semi-furnished, so I sold my bed and a few other pieces to Max's new roommate. She's just out of college and didn't have much of her own yet, anyway."

Wayne nodded, and Aunt Darla began puttering around the kitchen. "I was just about to start making some lunch, why don't we all have a bite before we head to town?"

"Sure," Jovie replied. She stood up to help, but Uncle Wayne stopped her.

"Wait, Jo, I've got something to show you," he began. "We've been going through a lot of stuff in the old barn and cellar, and there are some things I think you'd like to see."

Aunt Darla nodded her approval, shooing them away. Jovie changed direction, following Uncle Wayne with curiosity.

"I donated a lot of the items to the Historical Society in town about three years ago. You should drop by as soon as you get the chance; you'd love it. But a few weeks ago, I happened upon these," he said, stopping in the living room to open a tall, walnut storage cabinet.

He pulled out a shoebox, lifting the lid and exposing a stack of yellowed envelopes, tied with string. He took the papers out, along with a small velvet box. When he clicked the box open, Jovie gasped with delight. A vintage locket on a chain was lying inside, pewter with swirling filigree and a carved rose in the center.

"Oh, can I?" She held out her hand, and Uncle Wayne gently placed the necklace in her hand. Very carefully, Jovie opened the locket, revealing two tiny, antique pictures inside. On one side was a young man dressed in an old-fashioned suit. He had light hair and a beard, and, Jovie thought, a kind look on his face. The other picture was of four children, although it was difficult to make out much detail about them.

"Who are they?" Jovie asked.

"The locket belonged to your great-great-great grandmother, Elizabeth. The man is her husband, Frank, and those are their children. The oldest boy there is your great-great grandfather," Uncle Wayne replied.

"Wow," Jovie whispered, inspecting the pictures more closely. "And the letters?"

"Love letters between Elizabeth and Frank, written during their courtship and engagement," he answered.

"This is amazing," Jovie smiled at her uncle. "Can I borrow them? I'd love to sit and read through these!"

"Of course. I figured as much. Once you're settled in your place, stop by and see Miss Agnes at the historical museum. I'll bet she'd like to see them too, and she's got a whole display of the other things we donated. I'm sure she'd be pleased to show you," Wayne said.

"I'll do that," Jovie agreed.

Her stomach full of Aunt Darla's homemade tomato soup and Uncle Wayne's grilled cheese sandwiches, Jovie made the short drive from the ranch into town. Wayne and Darla followed her in their truck.

Jovie admired the fall foliage as she drove through the rolling hills of eastern Kansas, the fallow fields alternating with dense woods on either side of the winding road. Soon, she passed the city limits sign and made her way to Redbud Grove's Main Street.

The town square was a green, park-like space,

surrounded by the brick buildings of downtown businesses on all four sides. The town held gatherings and festivals throughout the year there, and a farmer's market on Saturdays from late spring to early fall. Park benches were scattered under the fiery maple trees and a gazebo stood in the center. A few people sat on the benches, enjoying the cool, sunny afternoon, and several kids played tag on the grass. Most of the shops and restaurants were open, and people milled about on the sidewalks.

Jovie hadn't been back to visit for a few years, and noticed that not much had changed since her childhood. She hadn't grown up in Redbud Grove. Her parents were rather adventurous, and had taken Jovie and her younger brother all over the world for various work opportunities. By the time she was five, Jovie had more stamps in her passport than most people did in their entire lives.

She didn't begrudge her parents her unusual upbringing. It was fun to see so many different places and meet all kinds of interesting people. However, it was always hard saying goodbye and having to make new friends all over again every few years. Still, Jovie felt thankful for the experiences that had shaped her into an independent, open-minded person.

However, her happiest memories had been visiting her aunt and uncle's farm, playing with her brother and cousins while the adults chatted over coffee and cake in Darla's homey kitchen. Redbud Grove had been the anchor in her ever-changing world, and she was glad it still felt like home.

∞∞∞

After a quick meeting with her new landlord, Jovie had the keys to her new apartment in hand. They fit into a nondescript, sturdy black door off the sidewalk, wedged between a flower shop and an insurance office. Unlocking the door, Jovie found that it immediately led to a stairwell, and she eagerly climbed up.

At the top, the landing opened to one large room that held the living, dining and kitchen spaces. Three walls were painted a crisp white, while the one that faced the square had been left as exposed brick. The original wood floors had been refinished, their lightness giving the space a cheery, open feel. A gray sofa with a matching arm chair and a small television made up the living area. There were two metal barstools at the kitchen counter, but no dining table in the small nook that overlooked the square. The kitchen was small, but freshly painted and clean. Crossing to the hall off the kitchen, Jovie found the two bedrooms with a single bathroom between, and a washer and dryer in a hall closet.

"I love it," she grinned, walking over to the brick wall and looking out over the square. Running her hand over her belly, she said, "It's perfect for us."

Wayne and Darla helped Jovie unload her car and carried the boxes upstairs. She spent the rest of the day unpacking and arranging her few decorative items to make the apartment homey. By the time darkness fell, she was exhausted. Her aunt and uncle left, making her promise to call if she needed anything, and Jovie fell into bed. She was asleep before her head even hit the pillow.

Chapter 3

The next morning was Sunday, and since Jovie hadn't bothered with setting an alarm, she slept in late. The busy previous day, combined with her pregnancy fatigue, had worn her completely out. Thankfully, since her second trimester had begun, the nausea had mostly subsided. It only seemed to rear its ugly head when she was hungry.

When she could no longer ignore her rumbling, uncomfortable stomach, Jovie reluctantly threw back the covers. She slipped into her fleece robe and slippers and padded out to the living space. The morning was chilly, and she bumped up the temperature on the thermostat to heat up the place.

Aunt Darla had offered to run out and buy some grocery staples yesterday, but Jovie had declined. Her hormones had given her very strong opinions on what sounded appetizing and what caused her to gag. This morning, however, she wished she had accepted Darla's help. As it was, her cupboards were rather empty except for a few snack-type foods she'd packed in her car for the trip.

Jovie grabbed an apple and a granola bar, settling down at the bar to eat while she made a grocery list. She pulled out her phone to make sure the store was in the same location as she remembered, and then hurried off to the bathroom for a quick shower.

Half an hour later, Jovie finished blow-drying her hair, smoothing her dark blond bob with her hands. She applied a few quick swipes of mascara and a little gloss to her lips. She surveyed her reflection in the mirror and shrugged. She supposed she needed to buy some maternity clothes soon, because nothing seemed to fit right.

Today she had thrown on another pair of black leggings and an oversized pink tunic that should have been flowy, but had become rather snug. She slid her arms into a thickly knitted, gray cardigan to ward off the chilly air. Max called it her "old man sweater," but Jovie loved it and, more importantly, it was comfortable. Slipping into some boots, Jovie tucked her grocery list into her purse and headed downstairs.

Two hours later, Jovie finished putting the rest of her purchases in the refrigerator and cabinets. She sank onto the couch with a plate of crackers and chicken salad she'd purchased from the grocery store deli. It had taken longer than she'd expected to navigate the unfamiliar layout, and now she was exhausted and famished.

Absentmindedly, she clicked the TV on and scrolled through the channels as she ate her lunch. *I could really use some old-school comedy right about now,* she thought. *Ooh, Jim Carrey, perfect!* Snuggling deeper into the sofa, Jovie was only five minutes into the goofy nineties movie when she slumped over, fast asleep.

When she woke up, Jovie's head was fuzzy and she felt a bit disoriented. Afternoon sunlight streamed in the windows and an obnoxious commercial for carpet cleaner blared out of the TV set. Rubbing her eyes and stretching, Jovie switched it off and headed for the bathroom. She splashed her face and tried to clear the cobwebs from her brain.

Maybe I should go for a walk. The fresh air would do me good, Jovie thought. Uncle Wayne had pointed out the historical museum they day before. She was certain it was closed today, but she could walk by and peek in the windows anyway.

Opening her front door, a blast of cool breeze hit Jovie in the face, waking her fully. Next week was Thanksgiving, and the weather had decided it was autumn at last. Walking briskly to stay warm, Jovie crossed the street and onto the green space of the square. The museum was directly across from Jovie's apartment.

The square was quiet and peaceful. Jovie realized that most of the shops were closed for the day. The redbud trees, for which the town was named, were barren now, but in the spring the square would be a riot of purple. Today, yellow, orange and brown leaves from stately maples and oaks crunched underfoot.

Crossing the street again, Jovie's eyes skimmed the brick buildings. A blue sign with black-painted letters advertised, "Redbud Grove, Kansas: Historical Museum" above a faded green door. Window displays on each side were decorated with antique memorabilia and bordered with white twinkle lights.

The shop next to the museum had a red-and-white striped awning and a few black iron café tables on the sidewalk. In the window, "Aggie's Café and Antiques" was written in swirling red letters.

Jovie assumed it was the same Agnes that Uncle Wayne had spoken of. She wished the café were open today. A nice cup of hot tea sounded wonderful. She leaned closer to see if the menu was visible from outside, so she'd know what to order when she stopped by the next morning.

Movement caught her eye. A light was on in the back of the café, and Jovie saw an elderly lady walking toward her. She jumped in surprise, but the lady smiled and waved, heading for the door. Turning a key in the lock, the glass door jingled with bells as she opened it.

"Hello, there," the elderly woman said. Her face crinkled in a friendly greeting, and Jovie felt herself smiling back. The lady was short and wiry, with thick, white hair that was curled and teased in the shape of her head. Her blue eyes were clear and sharp, and hot pink glasses hung around her neck from a gold chain, bumping against a snowflake-embroidered sweatshirt that matched her eyes.

"Hi," Jovie said. "Sorry to snoop; I was just trying to see the menu for next time you're open."

"You know what, I was just about to have a cup of tea. Would you like to join me?" The woman looked around conspiratorially. "Shh, don't tell anyone," she said, grinning cheekily.

"Um, sure. Are you the owner?"

"In the flesh. I'm Agnes Taylor, but most everyone calls me Aggie." She gestured to the sign in the window.

"I'm Jovie Campbell. Nice to meet you," Jovie shook her offered hand.

"Well, come inside and get warmed up, young lady. It's freezing out here," Aggie shivered and ushered her in, locking the door behind her.

Jovie paused a moment to take in the room. It was larger than it looked from outside. To the left was the café area, with several tables scattered around. They were all mismatched, but each covered with red-and-white checkered tablecloths. Past the tables was a counter to place orders. A large chalkboard hung high on the wall behind it, showcasing the food and drink menus.

Next to the counter was a glass case for baked goods, and behind the counter were several machines for making coffee and a swinging metal door that led to the kitchen in back. Agnes disappeared into the kitchen and a moment later, lights flickered on overhead.

To the right of the café and stretching to the

back of the building, antiques were arranged at tables and in booths. Decorative items were in the front, but Jovie could see some larger furniture pieces cluttering the back of the shop. She made a mental note to see if there was anything she could use for her sparsely furnished apartment.

Aggie reappeared, holding a small plate of cookies. She grabbed two cups from a shelf under the counter and flicked on an electric tea kettle.

"Have a seat, dear. I hope you don't mind—I always like a little something sweet with my afternoon tea. Oh, what kind of tea do you like? I have just about everything." Aggie gestured to a small cabinet with tiny, teabag-shaped drawers. "English breakfast, peppermint, chamomile, green with lemongrass and spearmint, earl grey, ginger peach, berry fusion…" Aggie continued to rattle off tea flavors.

"Ginger peach, please," Jovie replied, when Aggie stopped to take a breath. She nodded approvingly and moved to fill two mugs with the boiling water.

"Tell me about yourself, dear. You're new to Redbud Grove?" Aggie set a full tray down on the nearest table and motioned for Jovie to sit while she served her a steaming cup of tea and two cookies on a small plate.

"Thanks, this smells delicious. Yes, I just moved here yesterday, actually. How did you know?" Jovie took a tentative sip, careful not to burn her tongue.

"I know most everyone around here," Aggie replied, waving a hand in the air. "Besides, the gossip at the beauty shop yesterday was that Wayne and Darla Reynolds were spotted helping a young lady move boxes into Bud's vacant apartment," Aggie said, referring to Jovie's landlord. "The town's grown over the years, what with the university at the edge of town, but we locals are still pretty tight-knit."

"Word travels fast," Jovie said, and Aggie nodded. "Darla and Wayne are my aunt and uncle. I used to visit Redbud Grove when I was a kid. I found myself needing a fresh start, and this was best place I could think of," Jovie said. Her eyes flicked down to her belly.

"May I ask, how far along are you?" Aggie inquired.

"Eighteen weeks," she replied.

"Babies bring a lot of change, but it's of the best kind. Of course, I'm a granny, so I have to say that," Aggie winked. "I know it can be scary, though," she patted Jovie's hand reassuringly. "I sure didn't know what I was doing the first time around, and she turned out just fine. It really is true what they say about it taking a village to raise a child. And any friend of Wayne and Darla is a friend of mine."

"Thanks," Jovie replied softly, tucking a blond lock behind her ear.

"So, um, Uncle Wayne mentioned that he donated some things to the museum. I'd love to look at them sometime. Yesterday he gave me my great-great-great-grandmother Elizabeth's locket and a collection of love letters between her and her fiancé."

Aggie's eyes sparked with interest. "Oh, I'd love

to see those sometime, too! You know what, if you're not busy right now I can show you Kathleen's display. Just let me check my bread in back and grab the timer."

"Kathleen?" Jovie asked.

"Oh, that would be your...let's see...four times great-grandmother," Aggie called over her shoulder. Returning from the kitchen, she grabbed her teacup and headed toward the antique section and called for Jovie to follow. Weaving in and out of the booths, Aggie led her to a side door tucked behind the larger furniture. Unlocking it, she pushed it open and led her into the museum next door.

"Oh, they're connected, that's nice!" Jovie exclaimed.

Aggie nodded. "Many of these old buildings are. I lucked out that mine were among them. It sure makes my life easier." She felt around in the dark, nearly tripping over something in the process.

Jovie carefully balanced her tea with one hand while pulling her phone out of her back pocket and tapping the flashlight feature.

"Ah, clever," Aggie smiled. She finally found the light switch and flipped it on, illuminating the museum. It was larger than Jovie had anticipated from the modest window decorations.

Neat displays were arranged in a grid pattern, each having its own theme. Convenient descriptions were posted next to each display, explaining the items and for what they had been used. Jovie stopped to admire a turn-of-the-century dress hanging on a headless mannequin, but Aggie continued on, weaving in and out of the displays.

"Over here!" the elderly woman called. It was a history lover's dream and there was so much to see, Jovie knew she'd be back soon for a proper visit. For now, she scurried ahead to catch up with Aggie. Rounding the bend, she slowed to a stop as Aggie proudly stood by an area dedicated to nineteenth-century Kansas pioneers.

"All these items were donated by your aunt and uncle." Jovie's eyes roamed over the display, taking in the antique trunk, quilt, rifle, lamp, baby dress and kitchenware. Her gaze landed on a side table with a large Bible and a framed, black-and-white photograph of a woman with blond curls piled on her head.

Aggie carefully picked up the photo. "This was Kathleen, Elizabeth's mother," she explained.

"Wow," was all Jovie could say, as she gingerly took the photograph in her hands. She spent the next few minutes roaming the display, carefully fingering the old quilt and thumbing through the pages of the family Bible. Jovie had never been religious, but she reverently read the names of her ancestors in the spidery, old handwriting.

By the time her tour was over, Jovie thanked Aggie and was eager to get home and read the letters between Elizabeth and Frank. She promised to come back soon and bring them, so Aggie could have a look as well.

However, Jovie knew she needed to get some work done and organized for the upcoming week. Tomorrow she would be able to access Professor Black's office and she would begin teaching on Tuesday. Her stomach churned nervously at the thought of a classroom full of students to teach.

The professor had been undergoing chemotherapy treatments and it was becoming increasingly difficult for him to function. He had been recording as many lectures as he could from his home on good days, so the students could watch them in lieu of his absence, but they really needed someone in person.

Professor Black had emailed, and video chatted with Jovie several times in the last few weeks to bring her up to speed. He had extensive chemo, radiation, and surgery plans for the next several months, but he was well-organized and had left his past lesson plans in the office for her. Jovie was eager to refresh herself with the material and prepare for her first classes.

Agnes watched the young woman walk away from the café. She had kept Avery's secret since she disappeared three years before, and through some bizarre time-travel conundrum, she seemed to be the only one that remembered Avery with any clarity. Everyone else seemed to have a dim, fuzzy recollection of the young woman who had been her museum assistant. She'd had help off and on since, but she was currently without someone to assist her at the museum, and she found herself missing her young friend.

The two were miraculously able to communicate via letters in the secret trunk compartment, right in the middle of Kathleen's display which Jovie had been exploring. She wouldn't tell Avery's story, knowing Jovie would think her a crazy old lady, but she wished she could divulge her intimate knowledge of the family to this girl. She seemed so fascinated by their history. As it was, she'd offered little tidbits of insight as Jovie exclaimed over each item.

After they'd said their goodbyes and Jovie had gone home, Agnes walked back through the museum, ensuring all the lights were off before returning to the café. She was overcome with a strange feeling, not completely unlike déjà vu, but she couldn't put her finger on it. She wondered what it could mean, and if there were unexpected changes on the horizon yet again.

Chapter 4

Thanksgiving Day, 1890

A very mopped her forehead with the back of her hand as she loaded more dishes into the washtub. It had been a busy, lovely day with her husband, children, and their good friends and neighbors. However, it was hard work, and she was eager to finish and rest her aching feet.

The children had scattered outside, oblivious to the cold, and were playing hide-and-seek. Meanwhile, inside, all the adults were pitching in to clear up so that it would be done quickly. Lizzie had also offered to help, but Avery urged her to go outside and get some fresh air. She noticed her now, not joining in with the others but walking alone toward the woods.

Lizzie had been quiet lately, and that was rather contrary to her nature. She usually talked anyone's ear off that would listen. Avery worried about her oldest, seeing that she was struggling to find her place in life. She was not a child anymore, but also not quite an adult. Avery fretted, seeing the leadership potential in Lizzie and fearful that society would squash it out of her. She prayed they would have an opportunity to talk later.

As it turned out, they found themselves alone that evening. After the Johnsons had driven away in the darkening twilight, the younger children soon began to get very droopy-eyed. Jake and Avery put them to bed early after their busy day, and then he kissed her cheek and headed out to finish the evening chores.

Lizzie sat next to the fire, staring at a book but never turning the pages. She shifted in the rocker and sighed. Avery crossed the room and gently took the book from her hands.

"Want to talk about it?" she asked, sitting down. Lizzie's eyes were teary as she looked at the woman who had loved her as her own for a decade.

"I don't understand why...but I just feel absolutely wretched. I want to fly away and do something important, but I don't know what it is, and I just feel..." Lizzie trailed off as the tears streamed down her cheeks.

"Trapped?" Avery guessed, pulling her into a hug and dabbing her face with a handkerchief.

"Yes, that's exactly it. I don't want to get married yet, but I can't stay here forever! Men can go anywhere and do anything. Why can't I?"

Avery nodded in understanding. "I wish things were different for you, truly I do. But it won't always be this way, and you needn't let other's expectations dictate your life," she added.

"Ordinary girls may have few options, but you

are extraordinary, Lizzie. I've always known you would outgrow us and go on to do something very special. God has created you just as he wants you to be and given you your own gifts to use for his glory. Scripture says, '*For I know the plans I have for you,*' *declares the Lord. 'Plans for welfare and not for evil, to give you a future and a hope.*'"

"Jeremiah 29:11," Lizzie mumbled.

"Exactly," Avery said. "I know God has a plan for your life, but the unknown and waiting can be very difficult. We'll keep our eyes and ears open, okay? Your pa and I will help anyway we can, and I hope that you'll come to one of us if you need to talk. But it's so hard to be patient, isn't it?"

Lizzie nodded. Her spirits appeared to be lifted a bit, although her apprehension was still obvious. Avery trusted God knew all about the future he'd planned for Lizzie, and that she would discover it soon.

∞∞∞

November 2018

What a week! Jovie thought to herself as she trudged up the stairs to her apartment Friday afternoon, nearly two weeks later. She had not anticipated teaching would exhaust her so. Combined with the fact that yesterday had been Thanksgiving with her aunt and uncle, and she'd gone to the office today to plan next week's lessons, fatigue was quickly catching up to her.

Her welcome into the fold of academics had been mostly pleasant. There were a few quirky, socially awkward teachers, which didn't bother her in the slightest. One professor seemed downright rude, but she tried to brush off his callous remarks and clipped mannerisms and not take them personally.

Jovie was still getting used to being called "Professor Campbell," but she liked the ring to it. As the youngest teacher at the university, she tried hard to maintain the balance of being professional, yet also friendly and approachable for the students. Most of her students were freshmen and sophomores, so there was a big enough age and maturity gap that Jovie felt more like an authority figure and less like a peer. But compared to the other professors, she felt woefully inexperienced.

Professor Black had certainly left big shoes to fill. Everyone on campus seemed to adore him, which left Jovie wondering how she would measure up. He had given extensive notes on what needed to be covered for the remainder of the semester, of which only a few weeks remained. Jovie dove into the material eagerly and had spent many nights falling asleep studying her lesson plans.

Tuesday and Thursday were her busy days, with both American History classes meeting. Those classes lasted longer, since they only met twice a week. On Monday, Wednesday and Friday mornings she taught Western Civilization and Geography. When she wasn't teaching, she busied herself in the office tweaking lesson plans to her liking, grading papers, and organizing the space, although she wasn't a particularly tidy person. Though it was exhausting, Jovie found her work positively invigorating, and she marveled at her newfound sense of purpose as she dug into her studies for each class.

This week she'd only had classes on Monday and Tuesday because of the holiday. She spent much of Wednesday grading papers, and then baked a sweet potato casserole to contribute to her family's Thanksgiving feast.

Jovie's parents and brother weren't able to make it to the farm this year. However, her cousins had come home, and she'd had a wonderful time catching up with them. Michael was married and had two little kids, and Ben brought his new girlfriend home for the first time. They all stayed up until the wee hours of the morning playing cards and board games.

By the time Jovie finished grading papers and lesson planning Friday afternoon, she was dead tired and looking forward to a quiet weekend. She hoped to visit the museum and Aggie over the weekend. Jovie had popped into the café several mornings for tea on the way to work, but she hadn't had a chance to visit with Aggie besides a quick hello.

Jovie wearily set down her purse and heavy tote bag with her laptop and papers in the hallway. She made her way to the kitchen to make a turkey and hot roll sandwich with the leftovers Darla had sent. Once her belly was full, she decided a power nap was in order.

Two hours later, Jovie jolted awake. The quilt had fallen to the floor and she was chilly. Glancing at her phone, she checked the time. *3:30. Sounds like teatime,* she thought to herself. She'd adopted the tea habit as a teenager, when her family was living in England, and it had stuck into adulthood. However, she didn't really feel like getting out to the café. Instead, she threw on a fluffy sweater and padded to the kitchen, filling a kettle with water and setting it on the stove to boil.

While she waited, Jovie opened the shoebox she had left on the kitchen counter and pulled out the love letters between Elizabeth and Frank. She hadn't had a spare moment for more than a cursory glance at them since her uncle had given them to her. Carefully untying the string, she sifted through the stack, checking for dates. Someone had neatly arranged them in order, so she began reading the oldest one.

Jovie had read through three letters by the time the water was heated. She stepped into the kitchen to pour her tea. The letters were lovely. From what she could gather, Elizabeth and Frank had worked together and been friends for a long while.

She was fascinated by their jobs: they were employees of the Children's Aid Society in New York City, and they accompanied orphan children on their journey west to be placed in new homes on the frontier. Jovie wondered how Elizabeth, a Kansas farm girl, had come to land that sort of a job.

Sipping her tea, Jovie read through the remaining letters. They were filled with love and hopeful plans for the future the young couple was making. During one trip west, Frank had to stay in New York instead of accompanying Elizabeth and the children. They missed each other terribly. Jovie wondered what it would be like to feel that way about someone, and if she'd ever find out someday.

Other letters were simply written while they were both in New York, but forbidden to express their affection while working together. The letters were filled with their love for each other, and they shared a mutual concern for the children in their care. Jovie thought back through what she knew of the Orphan Train history and knew there were many heartbreaking stories associated with it.

She wondered how long Elizabeth and Frank worked with the Children's Aid Society, and how the experience affected their future. She knew they went on to marry and start their own family a short time after the letters were written. She'd have to ask Agnes about it tomorrow.

Setting down the last letter as she stood up and stretched, Jovie made her way over to the tall windows that overlooked the square. Darkness had fallen and most of the shops had closed for the day, except the handful of restaurants. A few twinkle lights were wrapped around the lampposts, bathing the square in a soft glow.

Tomorrow, Jovie planned to take the letters over and let Agnes have a look at them, as she'd promised. She wanted to meander through the museum again anyway, and she'd been meaning to check Aggie's furniture selection at the antique shop. She could really use a small dining table and a few odds and ends to make the apartment a bit homier.

Jovie's stomach grumbled loudly, and she giggled as she placed a hand gently on her belly. "All right, all right, I'll figure out dinner," she whispered. Grabbing her phone, she called a local pizza place and ordered a large sausage and pepperoni with green peppers. To make herself feel better for giving into her cravings so soon after a giant turkey dinner, she added on a side salad.

She missed Max. Friday night pizza had been their tradition for as long as she could remember. Setting down her phone, she moved to open her laptop. She could use a nice video chat with her old roommate while she waited for the pizza delivery.

∞∞∞

December 1890

Lizzie hurriedly unhitched the team and began watering and brushing down the horses. She had just returned from visiting her best friend, Grace, who had moved to into town after marrying a few months ago.

Grace's family owned the farm and ranch next to Lizzie's, and their fathers were partners in the cattle trade. But Grace's new husband needed to be close to the blacksmith's shop, where he worked with his own family's business.

Lizzie and Grace hadn't been separated by more than a hayfield most of their lives, and Lizzie missed her friend something awful. She couldn't help but feel like life was passing her by, with her friends moving on one by one. A visit into town had been just what she needed, yet it had been bittersweet.

Grace had been eager to show Lizzie how she was turning their small house into a home, as well as share the news that she was indeed expecting a baby. Lizzie had had her suspicions for a few weeks, and she was glad to share in her friend's happy news. They had celebrated by going to have coffee and pie at the local hotel.

Since the railroad had come to town a few years before, the small community of Redbud Grove had grown. There were now many more options for shopping and dining than in the tiny settlement they'd known as children.

Walking arm-in-arm with Grace back to her modest home, Lizzie was truly happy for her friend. Yet, the restlessness still stirred within her. The two women passed the station, and Lizzie's eyes caught a notice posted there. Another Orphan Train was set to come through town in a few months. The wheels turned in her mind and an idea began to form.

By the time she reached home, Lizzie's brain was buzzing with activity. She couldn't wait to talk to Avery. However, she was interrupted from her reverie when the barn door swung open and Noah entered. She groaned inwardly.

Noah had been working for her father for nearly

two years. The young man lived in the tiny cabin that Lizzie's parents had built when they first settled the homestead. Avery had also lived there during her short stint as their nanny and housekeeper, before she married Jake.

"Howdy, Liz," Noah said. He was the only person who referred to her by that name, and he knew it irked her.

"It's Liz-ZIE, cowboy," she corrected saucily. He held his hands up in mock surrender, his brown eyes laughing.

Lizzie knew he fancied her, he had made no secret about that. She'd figured out long ago that his merciless teasing was, in fact, thinly-masked flirting. She viewed him as nothing more than a brother and had told him as much. She hoped he would leave it at that.

"Can I help you with that?" Noah asked, taking the currycomb from her hand to finish brushing down the horse. Lizzie rolled her eyes and put her hands on her hips.

"Looks like you just did," she replied. She knew he was trying to be a gentleman, but sometimes his "helpfulness" got under her skin. He wanted the kind of woman who would be content to let him be the big, strong man, and her a happy homemaker with few thoughts in her head besides children and cooking hearty meals for him. That was certainly not Lizzie.

Of course, she wanted her own home and family, eventually. Being the oldest of six children, she had been quite maternal from a young age, and had taken over much of the family cooking as she'd gotten older. But that was just it—she had never been anywhere or done a thing on her own. And settling down in their little corner of the world before seeing anything else it had to offer, felt…disappointing, somehow.

Perhaps her pa and Avery had colored her ideas about men and women. Their relationship was different than the other marriages Lizzie had observed in their community. Avery had mentioned that she had extensive schooling in her younger years, having quite a good head for numbers and business sense. Once she became a part of their lives, she and Jake worked together to build their ranch. Where one excelled, he or she would take the lead in that area, and vice versa.

Avery had been their cook, housekeeper, and nanny when she'd first come to Redbud Grove. Her tender care had been a balm to the entire family, but they all still teased her about her kitchen mishaps. Although she'd made progress as a cook since then, Avery and Jake had eventually come to a compromise where they'd decided to split the kitchen and outdoor chores.

Lizzie didn't know any other mothers who would escape to roping cattle when she felt too cooped up in the house, or one that could be found poring over ledgers late at night because she was better at bookkeeping than her husband. Conversely, Lizzie didn't know many fathers who made such delicious apple crumble cake and flapjacks. Avery tended to always burn them, and had vowed to steer clear of them forever. On any given day, Jake was just as likely to be found in the kitchen as Avery was to be out milking cows or repairing the fence.

The arrangement was strange, but it worked for their family. Her parents had always been a team and expressed appreciation for one another frequently. In fact, sometimes their displays of affection at home became almost *too* much for their children's sensibilities. Not to say they never bickered; they certainly did. But for the most part, their unconventional home life was a happy one.

Lizzie sometimes wondered if she would ever find someone who measured up to the standard her parents had set. A man who wouldn't feel the need to cage her, but who was secure enough to give her the freedom to use the gifts that made her uniquely Lizzie.

She snapped back to the present and Noah's words. What was he going on about?

"Liz, I've been thinking. Things are going well with my job here at the ranch. I've a modest income, but it's enough to provide for a wife. Now, maybe you don't feel that way about me yet, but I think in time you'd start to. I'd be a good husband, honest. You'd be taken care of in every way. Plus, you could be right here with your family, just next door in the cabin!"

"What on earth are you talkin' about, Noah?" Lizzie croaked out. His burly, muscled frame stopped combing the horse, and he lifted his dark eyes to meet Lizzie's golden-brown ones. But there was no love reflected there. In fact, her tiny frame shook angrily as she ran her fingers through her brown curls in agitation. Not that he noticed, as he gathered his courage and spoke again.

"I'm saying I want to marry you, Liz. Will you be my wife?"

Lizzie felt shaken at his words and paused a moment before speaking. "So, you've got it all figured out, do you? Noah, I don't know how I can be any clearer. I don't feel that way about you. You're my friend, nothin' more. Plus, I'm all wrong for you. Have you ever once asked me what *I* wanted? No, you haven't, and that's not fair to me."

Lizzie sucked in a deep breath, willing herself to calm down. She managed to soften her tone a bit before speaking again. "It's not fair to you, either. You're a good man, and a hard worker. I'm sure you'll make someone a fine husband. But it can't be me. I'm far to strong-willed for the likes of you. We're not a good match, can't ya see that?"

"Lizzie, please. I love you." Desperation made him bold, and Noah stepped toward her, encircling her waist and pulling her to him. Lizzie froze for a moment, shocked into silence. She watched, horrified, as his face came closer to hers. Well, she'd never been kissed by a man, and he certainly wasn't going to be her first. She turned her head at the last second and all he caught was her ear, before she pushed him away with all her might. Her cold hand hit his cheek with a satisfying slap.

Hurt and anger flared in Noah's eyes, and Lizzie

felt as though she'd been punched in the gut. *He had no right,* she thought. *And I won't feel guilty about it.*

"Stay away from me, Noah," she said, finally finding her voice.

Noah nodded tersely, his hand rubbing his cheek. Clearly, he had expected that he could tame her fiery spirit and she'd eventually come to love him, even if she didn't now. She knew that wasn't true, and it would be unfair to both of them to pretend so. She turned on her heel and ran from the barn.

Chapter 5

2018

J ovie locked the front door behind her, stepping out onto the bustling sidewalk. It was mid-morning on Saturday, and folks were out Christmas shopping and milling around the square. The weather was beautiful, with clear blue skies, bright sunshine and just enough of a crisp chill to the air to warrant a jacket.

Jovie had finally ordered a few maternity clothes online, since there were no stores nearby for expectant moms. She mentally kicked herself for not shopping in the city when she'd had the chance.

For now, she'd make do with the package that had been delivered to her door earlier in the week. Self-consciously, she tugged at the tall band that stretched over her belly and was attached to her new jeans. Jovie smoothed the knitted, pale gray top over it. The shirt clung to her belly possessively, seeming to announce her news to the world. Jovie pulled her jacket more tightly around herself, adjusted her scarf, and headed across the square.

The bells jingling, Jovie stepped into the café first, deciding to grab a cup of tea before exploring the shop and museum. There were a few people enjoying late morning drinks and pastries scattered around the tables. Bud, her landlord, was having his coffee and grunted out a hello. He hadn't been overly friendly when they'd first met, but Jovie decided to classify him as a lovable grump, rather than a judgmental old man. She hoped, at least, and gave him a friendly smile.

A guy she hadn't seen before was working behind the counter, his back to her as he operated the espresso machine. During the week, she'd only seen Aggie and a middle-aged woman named Deb bustling around the place, and occasionally one of the students from her geography class.

He carefully turned, stepping out from behind the counter and delivering the drinks to two elderly ladies sitting by the window. Jovie nearly laughed out loud as she noticed he was wearing a red, dancing candy cane-emblazoned apron over his jeans and green flannel shirt.

He noticed Jovie's presence and gave her a friendly smile as he made his way back to the counter. She took off her jacket and scarf, hanging them on the coat tree provided near the door, and approached him.

"Hi, what can I get for you?" Deep blue eyes met hers, and Jovie just stared at him for a moment, searching for her voice. The man that had seemed so ordinary when she'd entered the café now seemed very handsome up close, in a rugged sort of way. His light brown hair was mussed, and he was average in height and build, but his rolled-up shirtsleeves revealed muscular arms. A bit of stubble grew along a strong jaw and he smiled, waiting for her reply.

Jovie gathered her wits about her, returning his smile and ordering English breakfast tea. "Festive," she remarked, gesturing to his apron.

"Oh, yeah. Gram's orders. She's the boss," he shrugged, chuckling as he took the cash she'd fished out of her purse. His hand brushed hers, and Jovie tried to ignore the thrill that shot through her own.

"Gram?" Jovie asked.

At that moment, Agnes appeared, emerging from the kitchen doors. "Ah, Jovie, I see you've met my grandson.

"Oh, I didn't realize," Jovie answered.

"My Gabriel," Aggie said proudly, patting his cheek as she switched the kettle on and rummaged under the counter.

Gabriel smiled, his cheeks reddening. "Just Gabe is fine," he said to Jovie.

"Jovie Campbell," she replied.

"Nice to meet you," he said, counting out her change and reaching for a bright red mug. "Have a seat anywhere you'd like, and I'll bring your order to you when it's ready."

Gabe turned away, trying not to gawk at the woman he'd just met, and busied himself preparing her tea. When she'd walked into the café, he'd heard the bells but didn't look up right away. But when he'd turned from Ellen and Marge's table and found her eyes on him, he was almost sure she'd heard his heart thundering from across the room.

Gabe didn't ordinarily find himself so stunned by a pretty face. But something about her bright eyes and rosy cheeks drew him to her instantly. Short hair framed her face with soft waves, and she'd looked around the café with a tentative smile on her lips.

He hadn't realized she was pregnant until she removed her jacket and scarf to approach the counter. He was surprised to find himself filled with disappointment that the beautiful young woman was off-limits. Of course, she'd have a boyfriend or husband. She was expecting a baby, after all.

Gabe had attempted to act casual and treat her in the same manner as any other customer. That hadn't stopped him from nearly forgetting how to make change once she'd placed her order, though. She was even more exquisite up close and her sparkling hazel eyes were incredibly distracting.

Gabe finished steeping Jovie's tea and added the small amount of milk she'd requested. As an afterthought, he took a small plate and added a raspberry cream cheese Danish. It was getting close to lunchtime anyway, and Gram would want to make room in the glass display case for fresh desserts soon.

"Here you go," Gabe said, setting down her tea

and Danish. He noticed no ring graced her finger as she curled her hands around the warm mug. Of course, that didn't mean anything. Lots of people didn't wear rings. Jovie saw the dessert and looked up at him in surprise.

"Oh, I didn't order—" she began.

"On the house," he cut her off, grinning like an idiot. "New customer special," he said quickly. *Real smooth, man.* She returned his smile.

"In that case, I never turn down sweets," she replied. The bells jangled again as a couple of customers walked inside.

"Let me know if I can get you anything else," Gabe said, dragging his attention back to his job.

There weren't many newcomers to their small town. The university brought a steady influx of college kids, but they nearly all moved on to bigger and better things after graduation. Most of the local people his own age he'd known his whole life. He had lots of friends among them, but it had been a long time since a woman had caught his eye.

He was curious about this Jovie Campbell and wondered what her story was. Gram had mentioned meeting her a few days ago and really seemed to like her. Of course, Gram liked most people and was especially welcoming to newcomers, so maybe it was just her natural bent toward hospitality.

Still, Gabe couldn't help thinking there was something special about the young woman. He studied her profile as she sipped her tea and watched the shoppers walking by the large glass window. Her phone buzzed, and she glanced down, tapping out a reply. He wondered who it was that had brought the smile to her lips.

Get a grip, man. What's the matter with you?

The sound of a throat clearing brought Gabe out of his reverie. An elderly gentleman was waiting to place his order, while Gabe stood there with his tray of dishes that needed brought to the kitchen. With one last glance at Jovie, Gabe returned to the task at hand.

∞∞∞

Jovie watched Gabe's retreating back. She mentally scolded herself. *Oh, no you don't. A guy is the last thing you need right now, even one as nice and good-looking as that. You have enough life changes to deal with right now, with the baby and your new job. You don't need any more complications. Repeat after me: No. Guys.*

Jovie turned away and took a sip of her drink. *Oh geez, he even knows how to make proper English tea.* She wondered how firm her resolve would remain if he smiled at her again.

You're going to be big as a house soon and learning how to care for a newborn in a few short months. It's not like he'd even be interested. Shaking herself, she turned her attention to her phone and responded to the text from Max.

A few minutes later, Aggie returned from the kitchen and breezed through the café, checking in on each table and making friendly chitchat with her customers. Jovie waved at the elderly lady.

"How are you today, dear?" Aggie approached the table, steaming mug of coffee in hand.

"Good...better now," Jovie smiled, sipping her tea. "I finished Elizabeth and Frank's letters. I brought them if you'd like to take a look," Jovie said, gesturing to the box resting on the table.

Aggie's eyes lit up. "Oh, I'd love that, sweetie! Are you going to be here for a little bit?"

"Yes, I was planning on checking out your antique shop and then browsing the museum."

"Great! I've got to get back to my office just now. After you've finished up here, if you wouldn't mind bringing them over with you, I can take a little break and have a look," Aggie said.

"Sure, that sounds good," Jovie replied.

"Ok, see you in a bit. Enjoy the Danish, it's my favorite," Aggie winked, and Jovie wondered if she'd seen the exchange with Gabe.

"It's delicious," Jovie said, taking another bite as Aggie wove her way to the museum door.

Jovie finished her tea and dessert, and then meandered over to check out the furniture and home décor. Much of it wasn't her style. But a round, wooden table that had been painted white caught her eye at once. It was surrounded by mismatched chairs of faded red, green, blue and yellow. It would fit perfectly into the nook of her apartment. Eyeing a few other decorative pieces, she then slipped through the open, adjoining door to the museum and to Aggie's office.

The elderly lady's hot pink glasses rested on her nose as she inspected a stack of papers on her desk.

"Ah, Jovie, dear," Aggie greeted, rearranging a few files and papers to make room on the desk. "I'm just dying to hear about these letters. What did you think?"

"They are truly a treasure," Jovie said, opening the box and handing the stack of envelopes to Aggie. "I find their lives so fascinating! Did you know Elizabeth worked with the Children's Aid Society, and that's where she met Frank? For several years they worked in New York and made annual visits across the country to help orphans find homes in the west."

"Really? How intriguing!" Aggie wrote something on a pad of paper next to her. "I've only recently learned the Orphan Train came through town several times before the turn of the century. I'm adding it to my list to research for new memorabilia."

Jovie pulled out the velvet box, opening it to reveal the locket. "And this is the necklace that belonged to Elizabeth. Uncle Wayne said this was Frank, and their children are in this picture. This boy is my great-great grandfather."

She handed the locket to Aggie, who held it gently, examining the pictures closely before clicking it shut. She traced her weathered hands over the rose design delicately, look of awe crossing her face.

"It's beautiful," Aggie said. "Thank you for sharing it with me. You'd better take this home and keep it in a safe place." She handed the locket back to Jovie, and she delicately placed it back into its case.

"I'd like to study their work more, when I have the time," Jovie continued. "I've been pretty busy getting up to speed with my classes."

Aggie wanted to know more about Jovie's new job, and they spent a few minutes chatting before Jovie left to explore the museum. Aggie promised to return the letters after reading them.

Jovie could have spent hours meandering the aisles, soaking up all the history contained in the displays. There were a few other people visiting the museum, with which she exchanged pleasantries, but it was otherwise quiet. Aggie had mentioned that much of their foot traffic came from visiting school groups, and teaching them about the local history was her favorite part of the job. She also assisted the occasional person with genealogy research, which she found fascinating. She could probably tell Jovie more about her own family history than even Uncle Wayne knew.

When her stomach began rumbling loudly, Jovie checked the time and realized she had missed lunch. Reluctantly, she knew she needed to get home to do some work. She went back over to the antique shop and café first. It was deserted, the lunch crowd having come and gone. She expected shoppers looking for an afternoon pick-me-up would start trickling in soon.

Jovie heard whistling coming from the kitchen. As she stood there wondering if she should ring the bell for service, Gabe stepped through the swinging metal doors and jumped, surprised at her sudden appearance.

"Hey," he greeted. "I thought you had left."

"I went over and chatted with Aggie for a bit, and then kind of got lost in the museum for a few hours. It's amazing," Jovie answered.

"Yeah, Gram's worked really hard to make the place what it is. She works too much, but she loves it."

"Well, you can definitely tell how much effort she's put in. Oh, and I was looking at the furniture and I think I'd like to buy that white table with the mismatched chairs. Can I do that here?"

"Sure, I'll grab the tag and ring it up for you," Gabe disappeared to the back and returned quickly. He carried the card that had been attached to the table with the price written on it. "Would you like it delivered?" Gabe asked as he punched buttons on a tablet to register the sale.

"That would be great," Jovie answered, running her card and signing her name on the screen.

"I close up at 5:00 today, so we'll be over shortly after, if that works for you." Gabe took down her information and Jovie waved goodbye as she walked across the square.

A few hours later, Jovie sat cross-legged on the living room floor, surrounded by stacks of papers. Grading essays wasn't her favorite part of the job, but a few students had a creative take on the assignment.

Many, though, were uninspired and she was starting to get tired and bored reading them.

She was nearly finished when the doorbell rang, causing her to jump. Pushing her reading glasses to the top of her head, she realized she'd lost track of time and it was already dark outside.

Jovie rushed downstairs, unlatching and opening the door to Gabe and an older man, who had the same strong jaw and kind eyes. Jovie wasn't surprised when Gabe introduced him as his father, Sam, and after shaking hands they went to unload the truck with her new furniture.

They made short work of carrying the dining table upstairs together as Jovie directed them to place it in the nook. Settling the chairs in place, Gabe took a look around the small apartment. Jovie felt suddenly aware of the mess of papers strewn about and sticky-note reminders scattered on the countertop.

"Busy working?" Gabe asked.

"Oh, yes, job hazard," she grinned. "I love the topic, but I've about had my fill of Civil War essays for a while."

"You're a teacher?" Gabe asked, and Jovie nodded.

"That's right, Mama said you were the new history professor. She took Dr. Black's place," Sam explained. "I'm sure Mama's just dying to pick your brain."

Jovie laughed. "Agnes and I share an interest in the local history, for sure. I explored the museum today and she borrowed a collection of letters from one of my ancestors."

"I think you're her favorite person right now, then." Gabe said. "She was poring over some old letters when I closed up the shop tonight."

Just then, Sam's phone rang, and he excused himself to answer it.

"Do you usually work at the café? I haven't seen you there before, and I'm becoming a regular. Aggie supports my tea habit," Jovie said to Gabe, smiling.

"No, normally I just help with deliveries. But Gram needed some extra holiday help and caught me in between jobs."

"What sort of work do you do?"

"Construction. Dad's a contractor, and I started working for him when I was in high school. A couple of years ago, I started my own business remodeling houses. It's good business in a town like this, with lots of historic homes in need of updating. But nobody wants their house torn apart at Thanksgiving and Christmas, so I just finished a job last week and don't start my new project until January."

Jovie smiled. She detected a hint of pride in Gabe's voice, but not arrogance. It suited him.

"What's up?" Gabe asked, as his dad returned, tucking his phone back into his pocket.

Sam's brow was furrowed with worry. "That was your mom. Gram's had a bad fall, thinks she might have broken something. The ambulance is on its way," Sam said.

"Oh, no!" Jovie gasped. Aggie was so spry it was

hard to imagine her hurt and helpless.

Gabe and Sam said their hasty goodbyes and jogged downstairs, and Jovie locked up after them. She pulled out the leftover pizza and sat down at her new dining table, but it was hard to enjoy thinking about Aggie's injury.

From her seat, the windows looked out over the town square. She could hear the wail of the ambulance. A moment later, flashing lights illuminated the park, filtering through the trees and breaking the peacefulness of the otherwise quiet street. Jovie moved closer, pressing her nose against the large window, but she couldn't see well from so far away. A few minutes later, the ambulance sped down the street and the sounds of the siren faded into the distance.

Chapter 6

The next morning, Aunt Darla and Uncle Wayne stopped by after church to invite Jovie to lunch. She'd slept in and been lazy all morning, so she was ready to get out of the house for a while with her favorite aunt and uncle.

They walked to a barbecue place not far from Jovie's apartment, and over brisket sandwiches and coleslaw, Jovie shared the highlights of her classes and students. She told them about sharing the letters with Aggie and asked if they had heard anything about her accident.

"Oh yes, Miss Agnes was on everyone's mind this morning. She broke her hip and is going to need surgery to repair it. She'll be down for a while healing and doing physical therapy," Darla answered.

"Oh, no!" Jovie exclaimed.

"Although, the doctors probably have a tougher job trying to keep her sitting still than she'll have recovering," Wayne said. "It's a busy time of year for Agnes, and she's not going to be very happy to be sidelined."

"Why, what's she have going on?"

"The town puts on a winter festival every year before Christmas, and the Historical Society holds their annual fundraiser during the festival," Darla replied.

"Hmm," Jovie said, picturing Aggie trying to organize everything from a hospital bed.

They moved on to discussing the letters, as Uncle Wayne wanted to hear Jovie's thoughts on them, and the afternoon passed quickly. All too soon, she was back in her apartment and preparing for the week.

∞∞∞∞

A few days later, Jovie headed to her first doctor's appointment at Redbud Grove Medical Center after finishing classes for the day. There weren't many practitioners from which to choose in the small town, but Jovie had settled on visiting Dr. Schaffer, a family practice doctor who did everything from delivering babies to setting broken limbs. Aunt Darla had raved about her, and that was good enough for Jovie.

The office was small and quiet, with white linoleum floors and nature photos lining the walls. Silver tinsel hung from the windows and the check-in desk, and a small tree was lit in the corner. Christmas music played as Jovie filled out extensive medical history paperwork, and soon she was called back to an exam room.

After a rather curt nurse weighed her and took her vitals, Jovie felt the tension mounting within her. The wall clock ticked loudly and the paper on the exam table crinkled uncomfortably. She felt her nerves winding tighter and tighter until she thought they'd snap. Finally, Dr. Shaffer came in.

Jovie breathed a sigh of relief. The middle-aged woman's friendly, yet professional, manner put her at ease immediately. She answered Jovie's questions patiently and asked a few herself before measuring Jovie's belly and pulling out the Doppler to listen to the baby's heartbeat.

Jovie felt herself relax further as she heard the familiar steady, whooshing sound. Dr. Schaffer smiled back. "About 150 beats per minute," she said a moment later. "Everything looks perfect."

Jovie scheduled her next appointment, at which she would have an ultrasound to take measurements and find out the baby's sex, if she was so inclined. She felt giddy with excitement and even stopped at a children's boutique on the way home to browse baby items.

There was a plethora of adorable clothes, blankets, and nursery decorations in the shop. However, with the myriad of choices and realizing how ill-prepared she was, Jovie soon left the boutique feeling overwhelmed. She made a mental note to write out a list of baby items she'd need before attempting shopping again. Instead, she popped into the flower shop next door to her house. Fresh plants and greenery had always calmed her.

After being greeted by an apron-clad woman, Jovie selected a sweet arrangement of bright pink, purple and yellow flowers. She asked that they be sent to Aggie's hospital room. And just to cheer up her sparse apartment, she chose a small bouquet of dainty white flowers for herself.

"Are you new to town?" The florist asked as she rang up the order. "I never forget a face, and I don't think I've seen you in here before."

"Yes, I just moved here a few weeks ago," Jovie said. "Still getting settled in and trying to make the place feel like home," she gestured to the bouquet.

The florist smiled at her. She looked to be just a few years older than Jovie herself. "Welcome to town. I'm Sadie, by the way. Seems like you already know Mrs. Taylor?"

"My name's Jovie. Aggie was the first friend I made here," she smiled.

"She's such a sweet lady. I hope she recovers quickly," Sadie said, handing Jovie the receipt and the small bouquet. "Here you go. We'll have the arrangement delivered to Aggie first thing in the morning."

"Thanks," Jovie replied, exiting the shop with a friendly wave and jingling of bells on the door.

1890
Lizzie ducked past her bustling family down-

stairs and made a beeline straight for her room, hop-ing everyone would leave her alone. She shared a room with all the girls, but they had all been other-wise occupied downstairs. She threw herself onto the double bed she shared with Hannah, finally allowing the tears to fall and darken the pillow beneath her.

Lizzie's emotions were a tangled knot within her. She feared it could never be untied. She knew most of the girls in town would have scolded her for scorning Noah's proposal. They saw him as quite a catch of a husband. Lizzie, however, wanted nothing more than to escape, and shuddered at the thought of his arms around her.

The Orphan Train idea from earlier in the day seemed utterly ridiculous now. Lizzie had planned to ask Avery if she was in contact with anyone from the Children's Aid Society anymore. They had coord-inated Lily and Matt's adoption a few years ago, and Lizzie knew that both men and women traveled with and cared for the children as they came west. The re-mainder of the year, they worked in orphanages in New York.

Lizzie had foolishly allowed herself to dream that perhaps she could be one of those women. She had always had a knack for helping little ones who were hurt or scared, and the thought of traveling far away to a big city was exciting. However, she could see now that it was foolish to hope for something so far out of reach.

Her sobs abated, followed swiftly by a throb-bing headache. Lizzie crossed to the washbasin, dabbing at her flushed cheeks with a cool cloth. Quietly opening the door, Lizzie tiptoed across the hall to her parents' bedroom. There weren't many items on the simple wooden dresser, and Lizzie soon found what she sought. She picked up the black-and-white photograph of her mother, Kathleen.

Unlike Drew and Caroline, who were so young when their mother passed, Lizzie remembered her mama. As she had gotten older, though, her memories had faded into a blurry, dream-like quality.

If she concentrated hard enough, she could still remember the sound of her mama's laugh and the way her blond curls always escaped their pins. She carried herself with a proud tilt of her head as she walked arm-in-arm with Pa, admiring the homestead they were building.

Lizzie closed her eyes, willing the memories to bubble up to the surface. Her mother's embrace had always smelled of roses and apples, mingled with earth from the garden—a perfect representation of how Lizzie remembered her mother. Sweet, but grounded in the reality of life on a farm.

Setting the photograph back onto the table, Lizzie ran her fingers over Avery's small jewelry box and landed on the leather book next to it. The journal had belonged to Kathleen and chronicled her life from the time she set off west as a new bride until her death a few years later.

Avery used to read passages aloud to the children, hoping to keep the memory of their birth mother alive. After she married Jake, he encouraged her to write down her own journey and thoughts about her new life. Lizzie had seen Avery write in the journal often in those early years, though she hadn't much lately.

Carefully, Lizzie picked up the book and took it back to her room. Surely Avery wouldn't mind now if she read some of her mother's entries. After all, it was all she had left to remember her by.

Truthfully, that was all Lizzie intended to do. But as the hours passed, she became more and more engrossed with her family's story. When Caroline came up to ask if she was coming to supper, Lizzie turned her down and kept reading. And although she felt rather guilty, she didn't stop at her mother's last entry. Curious, Lizzie read on as the handwriting changed from her mother's narrow scrawl to Avery's loopy style.

Smiling, Lizzie read of Avery's joy as a new bride to Jake, and of her love for him and the children. She'd jotted down little anecdotes of the children's funny escapades and the practical jokes Jake loved to play on her.

Lizzie recalled her eight-year-old self, and her certainty that God had dropped Avery right into their lives, seemingly out of nowhere. Avery had always remained somewhat vague about her life before coming to live with the Coles, and as a child, Lizzie hadn't thought to question it.

As she read on, Lizzie began to feel as if she were putting together pieces of a puzzle. Avery's entries sometimes held curious references to "the future," as if they were shards of her past. There was one passage in which Avery was mourning the anniversary of her parents' death in a car crash. *What is a car?* Lizzie wondered.

Feeling more and more like a snoop, Lizzie skimmed over the passages detailing Avery's heartbreak each month that passed without conceiving a child of her own. Her eyes caught the sentence *I wonder if my troubles becoming pregnant have less to do with me and more with preserving the timeline from which I came. If so, I will have to trust that God knows what he is doing, and that he is not punishing me. I should know by now that God has a perfect plan...in his own time.* That was downright curious.

In other passages, Avery referred to her friend Aggie and her amazement that they were able to send one another letters. Lizzie thought that was a rather odd thing to be excited about. She had often noticed Avery penning notes to her old friend Agnes and had assumed it was someone back east. She'd never thought to notice whether or not those letters were in the stack of mail to be taken to town.

The secret compartment of the trunk continues to be a miraculous line of communication with Aggie. When life feels overwhelming or I miss the conveniences of home, I feel a deep sense of joy and peace that my old friend still shares her wisdom with me, and it is a comfort to hear news from her life.

Lizzie's heart slammed in her chest. Straining to hear her family downstairs, she knew it wouldn't be long before they would start readying for bed.

She quickly dashed across the hall again. This time, she purposefully made a beeline to the trunk at the end of the bed. Throwing the top open, she rifled through the layers of quilts and clothing until her hands brushed the bottom. Fumbling with the boards, finally a loose one gave way. Breathlessly, Lizzie reached into the concealed hole, but her fingers touched nothing.

Sighing, Lizzie replaced the board and moved to put everything back, when her hand bumped the edge of a small box. Lifting it out, she flipped the lid open and a stack of folded papers fell out. All were filled with odd handwriting on faded blue lines, and there were three strange, perfectly circular holes on the left side of each page. And each letter was signed: *Love, Aggie.*

Lizzie worked to steady her breathing in the darkness. Her fingers itched to grab the box of letters she'd hidden under her bed, but it would have to wait until her sisters were sound asleep. Lily's breathing had already evened out, but Hannah flopped next to her like a fish. Caroline hadn't started snoring yet, so Lizzie waited impatiently.

Although Lizzie stilled her body, her mind was racing as she tried to figure out exactly what those letters might mean. She tried to push Avery's concerned face from her mind. Not long after finding the box of letters, her siblings had begun to trickle up-stairs to bed, so Lizzie stashed her find and tried to act normally.

She suspected Drew already knew about Noah's proposal, when he caught her eye as he bid her good-night. He raised his eyebrows in question, but Lizzie just shook her head. She didn't want to talk about it, and she certainly didn't want to bring up the near-kiss. If he knew the truth of that, he'd throttle Noah for sure.

Drew had simply hugged her silently, holding her a bit longer than usual. Of all her siblings, he was the one who would keep such information to himself. For once, Lizzie was glad for Drew's quiet demeanor.

When Jake and Avery had come upstairs to tell the children goodnight, they both looked at her worriedly and asked if she wanted to discuss any-thing. However, Lizzie had asked to be alone and they granted her space. They knew during the rare times when Lizzie wasn't talkative, she was deeply con-templating something and eventually would come to them, once she'd worked it out in her own head.

After what seemed like hours, a peace finally settled over the room as all three of her sisters slum-bered. Lizzie quietly crept out of bed and reached for the hidden box. She tiptoed to the small table and lit a candle. The room was quite crowded with the two double beds, but there was a lone rocking chair nes-tled in the corner, leftover from Hannah's baby days.

Settling into the chair, Lizzie strained to read Aggie's letters by candlelight. Much of it was just one friend sharing news with another—family members marrying or having a child, a longtime neighbor moving away, and a new pastor coming to minister at the church. Other bits of information were confusing—references to Kathleen's journal, the past, or the future. And still others made Lizzie wonder in what kind of town Aggie lived: she herself owned and ran two businesses, and there were references to her female friends or family members who were involved in all sorts of strange-sounding employ. But the most alarming thing was the date written at the top of each letter. According to the papers, Aggie lived over a hundred years into the future.

Bit by bit, Lizzie put all the pieces together. In the light of day, it would have been a ridiculous notion and she probably would not have entertained such thoughts. But something about the firelight flickering in the darkness made her believe that anything might be possible.

Once all the letters were read and Lizzie was going back over several passages in the journal, she reached a conclusion: against all odds, it seemed that her stepmother had traveled to the past ten years ago and had never returned to the future. Even stranger, all evidence pointed to her own mother's journal being the catalyst that brought Avery to them.

Lizzie paced the floor in front of the fireplace.

Unable to keep still after her realization, she had tiptoed downstairs, careful to avoid the boards that creaked loudly. An idea began to form in her mind. It was madness, of course, but her curiosity was getting the better of her. She wanted nothing more than to escape her current situation. Could she possibly wield the journal, and escape to a future that seemed much brighter than her world? Just to see what it was like. Of course, she'd come right back. Her family never need know she was gone.

Once the idea took root in her mind, it grew until there was no going back. Lizzie's mind was made up. But how could she use the journal? She gripped the book tightly in her hands and wished with all her might to go to Avery's future. Nothing happened. Lizzie's eyes darted toward the stairs.

"I wish to visit this future of which Avery writes," she whispered in the darkness. She felt ridiculous as her surroundings remained unchanged. Lizzie tried everything she could think of, to no avail. Finally, she tiptoed upstairs, frustration stinging her eyes. She climbed back into bed, clutching the book to her chest as the tears flowed soundlessly. Eventually she drifted off to sleep, wishing things could be different.

Chapter 7

December 2018

J ovie meandered down the sidewalk on a Friday morning, window shopping and taking in the cold, fresh air. Finals were over, and she had worked every evening grading her students' tests. With the exception of entering final grades, which she would do next week, the semester was over and winter break had officially begun.

That morning, as she ate a stack of pancakes at her new dining table, Jovie had cracked open a new notebook and started a list of things she needed to buy or prepare for the baby. There was so much to do, and she jotted questions in the margins to ask the more experienced women in her life. It was overwhelming, but she felt better having made some sort of a plan.

The notebook with its half-finished list bumped around her tote bag as she walked. Sadie, the florist, looked up from the bouquet she was arranging in the shop window, and waved. A few passersby nodded and said hello. She was beginning to recognize familiar faces in the small town.

Eventually, she found herself in front of Aggie's, and she eagerly entered the café. The warm, rich scent of coffee and spices surrounded her as she shed her coat and hung it up.

There were only a few patrons inside and nobody at the register as she approached. Jovie leaned over the counter to inspect a glass case of donuts, when suddenly Gabe's head popped up right in front of her. They both let out startled yelps at meeting face-to-face so suddenly.

"Oh, gosh, you scared me!" Jovie pressed her hand over her chest, her heart thumping wildly.

"Sorry, I didn't see you," Gabe grinned, and Jovie matched his smile. Today his apron was bright blue and decorated with bedazzled snowmen.

Jovie hadn't seen Gabe since Aggie's fall, and after ordering her tea, she asked how his Gram was doing.

Gabe rolled his eyes. "She's recovering well from the surgery, but she hates being laid up in bed. My family's taking turns staying with her, and she may or may not be driving them all crazy with her restlessness. She's making endless lists and delegating her responsibilities among all of us." He shook his head.

"I heard she organizes the Historical Society fundraiser," Jovie said.

"Yep. Guess who got nominated to be the new chairperson for that?" Gabe pointed both thumbs at himself, but smiled good-naturedly.

"Gram had most of the events planned already, but I've still got to get a move on making sure everything's lined up the way she intended. She's very particular. Winter Festival starts in a week, and the fundraiser Gala is a few days after that," he finished.

After chatting a few more minutes, Gabe headed back to the kitchen and Jovie took her tea and sat down at a table. She pulled out her list and her phone, connecting to the café's Wi-Fi and searching online for baby essentials. Good grief, did one baby really need so much stuff? She added "sleep sacks" to her list, whatever those were.

Jovie didn't even want to think about how much it was going to cost to purchase everything the baby would need in just a few short months. True, she had her nest egg, but now that she'd have a child to care for, she'd prefer not to blow it all before the baby even arrived. Her university salary was paid monthly, so she had to budget and stretch every penny carefully. And she'd already refused Parker's money. She didn't want anything from him.

Meanwhile, lunchtime patrons trickled into the café. The morning sun had given way to clouds, and a cold drizzle drove more customers than usual inside. Gabe ran back and forth taking orders, ringing up bills, and delivering food and drinks to everyone's tables, along with handling the occasional antique store purchase.

He was friendly with the customers, but Jovie noticed he had a frazzled look about him. A couple seated next to Jovie began to complain loudly about the long wait for their food.

Curiously, Jovie approached Gabe at the counter. "Hey, Gabe, is anyone working the kitchen today? Where's Deb?"

Concentrating on the latte he was crafting, Gabe replied, "Texas. She's had this big family trip planned for months, so I couldn't ask her to stay. Alex and Becca, the students who work here part-time, have gone home for Christmas, and the kid Gram thought she had lined up quit unexpectedly. My mom usually helps in the kitchen when we're short-handed, but she's taking care of Gram, so it's just me today."

"Time to call in some reinforcements, huh?" Jovie replied. She chewed on the inside of her cheek, thinking. "You know, I worked at a coffee shop in college," she began.

Gabe finally raised his blue eyes to meet hers. "You're hired!" he blurted.

Jovie laughed.

"No, I'm serious," he said. "Gram told me to hire some holiday help, I just haven't had a moment to get the word out. Are you done with classes for the year?"

Jovie nodded and thought about her current financial situation. She wasn't desperate, but she could use the extra money. Now that the university was on winter break, she had the time. She'd still need to do some work to prepare for next semester, but she could manage both.

"What do you say? Are you interested?" Gabe looked at her hopefully.

"It's a deal," Jovie nodded, smiling when Gabe shook her hand.

The whiny couple loudly asked again when their order would be ready. "One moment, folks!" Gabe disappeared into the kitchen. Jovie heard the ding of a timer and the clang of plates, and when Gabe came back he quickly delivered their sandwiches.

"Finally!" the man huffed, and Gabe apologized for his wait. Waggling his eyebrows at Jovie, Gabe grabbed a green apron with gingerbread girls dancing across the front and tossed it to her. "Can you start immediately?"

Lizzie's cheek pressed against something cold and hard. She felt icy water seeping into her clothes uncomfortably. Forcing her eyes open, her vision blurred as they tried to focus. There were unnaturally bright lights intermittently scattered around, piercing the darkness that surrounded her. It was very disorienting.

Where was her bed? Lizzie was quite certain she had fallen asleep in her room. Yes, she had been crying and holding her mother's journal. She was vaguely aware now that she was outside, and it was still nighttime, but the air didn't smell quite right. *How in the world did I get here?* she wondered.

Lizzie pushed herself to a sitting position, looking around. Brick walls were on either side of her, reaching up to touch the night sky. The stars seemed dimmer than usual, but perhaps that was because the sky was somewhat overcast.

A large, metal boxlike contraption was pushed against one brick wall. A foul odor wafted from it, and Lizzie could see several more lining the walls in the distance. Black iron landings and staircases crisscrossed up and down the sides of the buildings. Lizzie looked down the lane. It appeared that the hard, wet surface beneath her was a narrow street of some kind. It intersected with another street a short distance away, which was illuminated by a curious light atop a giant pole. More lights twinkled in the distance, shining down the street and lighting up windows.

Lizzie scrambled back in alarm as a moving object on wheels sped past, underneath the light thing. *What was that?* her mind screamed. It reminded her of a shiny, sleek metal buggy, but there were no horses pulling it—it seemed to move of its own accord.

As Lizzie shifted her position, she noticed her curious clothing. She was no longer in her warm, flannel nightgown. Tall boots stretched up her legs and over trousers that felt far too tight for her liking. She wasn't a man, after all. A long sweater fell loosely down to the middle of her thighs, and she pulled the black coat she wore around herself more tightly. Her hand caught on something, and she saw that her mother's journal was tucked into the coat pocket.

A terrifying sound pierced the darkness as another, larger moving buggy flew past with red and blue flashing lights. At the same time, a door opened in the wall nearest her. A column of light spilled out, and the voice of a young woman reached her ears. She was turned away from Lizzie, speaking to someone still inside. Lizzie couldn't make out her face, but her figure was illuminated against the bright light. She wore no jacket, and Lizzie could spot an expectant mother a mile away. The rounded belly protruding from the lady was a dead giveaway.

The woman held a large bag of something, which she turned and tossed into the metal box. Only then did she notice Lizzie, sitting on the ground and hugging her knees to her chest in fear.

∞∞∞

Jovie replied to Gabe's question as she opened the door to take the trash to the alley. It had been a very busy day, but she felt satisfied with the work they'd done. She and Gabe made a pretty good team. He was more familiar with prepping the food in back, so he'd done most of the cooking while she took over the barista and register duties.

Gabe gave her a crash course for each of the machines, and after a few mishaps, Jovie slipped into the familiar motions of crafting lattes, mochas and espressos. They had slipped into easy conversation through the day as they worked together, like old friends.

It was easier to have her hands and mind busy when she was near him. She'd hardly had time at all to think of how distractingly blue his eyes were. Almost, anyway. Now, the café was closed, and they were cleaning up for the night.

Jovie turned back toward the door after tossing the trash in the dumpster, but a flash of eyes in the darkness surprised her. She sucked her breath in, startled to see a person sitting in the middle of the alley. A young girl was curled up into a ball and visibly shaking.

"Hi, there," Jovie said softly, trying not to frighten the girl even more. Bending to prop the door open with an extra brick on the stoop, she tentatively stepped into the alley. Jovie bent down to her eye level.

"What are you doing out here in the cold?"

"I...I don't know," the girl's voice was barely a whisper.

Jovie's brow wrinkled in confusion. Strange. Had the girl been through something terrible? She wondered if she should call the police.

"Are you hurt?" Jovie asked. The girl shook her head slightly. "Well, we're just closing up, but I'm sure we could get you a nice hot cup of tea, or coffee, if you like. What do you say? Come on in and warm up; it's freezing out here."

Jovie stood and took the girl's icy hand, and she stood shakily. Leading her inside, the warmth and aromas of bread and coffee surrounded them. Jovie hoped it instilled a sense of safety and calm into the frightened girl. Their unexpected guest held her arms around herself and squinted her eyes from the sudden, bright light of the kitchen. Gabe's back was to them at the sink and he loudly banged the pot he was washing in the basin, causing the girl to jump.

"Don't worry, that's just my friend. He works here too," Jovie said, working to keep her tone soothing. "Gabe, we have a visitor. Can you put the kettle back on?" Turning and seeing they had company, Gabe's eyes were full of questions. Jovie shook her head slightly. *Not now.* He gave the girl a friendly smile and said hello, before disappearing through the swinging doors.

Following him, Jovie led the girl through the kitchen and to a chair in front. On the way, she grabbed some towels from the shelf under the counter. The girl took them gratefully and began dabbing the water off her face and hands.

"How about some nice chamomile tea?" she asked, and the girl nodded once again. "Be right back," Jovie said.

Jovie went and fetched a mug and tea bag, while Gabe reached for the boiling kettle and poured for her.

"What's going on?" he whispered, as Jovie carefully stirred honey into the tea.

"Not sure. She was just sitting in the alley, looking super freaked-out. She said she wasn't hurt, but..." Jovie risked a glance over her shoulder and found the girl watching them curiously.

Attempting a serene smile, Jovie approached the girl, placing the tea in front of her. Sitting next to her, she said, "Here you go. I'm Jovie, by the way. And that's Gabe. What's your name?"

"Lizzie Co—Lizzie…Jacobs," the girl replied.

"Nice to meet you, Lizzie," Gabe smiled, seating himself next to Jovie.

"Can you tell me what happened in the alley?" Jovie asked gently.

"Well, I—I don't remember," Lizzie shook her head, curling her hands around the hot mug.

"We can take you to the doctor, if you need," Gabe put in.

Lizzie looked slightly alarmed. "No, no need for that, thank ya."

"Is there someone we can call for you, then?" Jovie asked. The girl took a sip of tea, her brow furrowed.

"No, I'll be fine. Thank you. I don't know anyone here. Except—my stepmother used to know a woman who lived here. Her name is Agnes, I think. My stepmother always called her Aggie, though. Have you heard of her?"

"Aggie Taylor?" Gabe smiled. "Yes, it just so happens that she's my grandmother, and you're sitting in her café."

Lizzie's eyes brightened, and she sat up straighter. "Honest? Is she here right now?" She glanced around the darkened corners of the café.

"No, Gram's in the hospital right now, recovering from surgery. But once she's feeling a little better, I'm sure she'd be happy to visit with you."

Lizzie's face fell. She nodded, sighing, and took a sip of her tea. Jovie and Gabe exchanged glances, unsure what to do.

"Where are you staying? We can take you to your hotel." Gabe offered.

"I—I don't have a room yet," the girl replied.

Jovie watched her closely as Lizzie warmed her hands around her mug, her glance darting around the dimly lit room. She still seemed frightened, though not panicked as before. She didn't have any luggage, not even a purse. Perhaps she was a runaway? She looked young enough to be in high school. Long brown hair fell over her petite frame, frizzing slightly in the dry, warm air of the café. Golden-brown eyes met Jovie's gaze, and there was something very innocent about them.

Jovie's hand slipped subconsciously to her belly. What would she want someone to do if it were her child? Jovie had a feeling if they called the police, the girl would take off, and who knows what kind of trouble she'd get into.

Taking in a deep breath, Jovie said, "Listen, I just live across the square. You're welcome to stay at my place for the night. It's nothing fancy, but you can get into some dry clothes and sleep on the sofa bed. In the morning, we can figure out a plan. What do you say?"

Gabe's head jerked up, his eyebrows raised in surprise. Ignoring him, Jovie turned to the girl, whose face had brightened considerably. "I don't want to be any trouble..." Lizzie began.

"Don't worry about it," Jovie replied. "Really, it's fine. Honestly, I'd enjoy the company, especially on a night like this. There's a storm coming." Just then, lightning flashed, and a crack of thunder shook the café. The lights flickered.

Wide-eyed, Lizzie turned back to Jovie. "I'd be much obliged."

Rain began to pelt against the café's large windows. "I'll drive you. You don't want to walk home in this," Gabe stood up. "Jovie, will you give me a hand? Let's close up real quick before the electricity goes out."

"Sure thing. We'll be ready to go in just a few moments," Jovie said, and Lizzie nodded.

As soon as she passed the swinging doors, Gabe turned on her. "Are you crazy?" he whisper-shouted at Jovie. "You don't know anything about her! What if she's, like, a serial killer?"

Jovie tried to keep a straight face, but a giggle escaped. "Seriously, Gabe? She's a scared little girl. I'll be fine, promise. Also, I have pepper spray, if that makes you feel any better."

"I'm just not sure this is the best idea. Don't you think the police would be better equipped to help her?"

Jovie shook her head. "You didn't see her face, sitting out there in the alley. She was completely terrified. Whatever her problems are, they'll still be here in the morning, but she'll be able to think with a clear head once she's had a good night's sleep and some food."

Gabe hesitated, then nodded in acquiescence. "Okay, good point. I trust your judgment, but still...

be careful, okay? Put away anything valuable and lock your door when you go to bed."

"I'll be fine," Jovie said confidently.

A few minutes later, they all sprinted into the torrent to Gabe's waiting truck. Jovie jumped into the dry vehicle quickly, while Lizzie stared at it in wonder for a moment. Gabe finally yanked the back door open and helped her in.

Jovie glanced around the truck from her front passenger seat. In her hands, she held a worn, flannel shirt that had been tossed across the seat, as well as book with dog-eared pages. She glanced at the title: *Out of the Silent Planet* by C.S. Lewis. *Interesting,* she thought. Of course, Jovie had heard of Lewis' children's books, but this appeared to be some kind of space fantasy.

The truck was otherwise tidy, with a large toolbox sitting along the bench seat next to Lizzie. The girl was pulling her seatbelt in and out as if she'd never seen one before. Jovie absentmindedly pointed out the buckle as she inhaled deeply. Gabe's truck smelled like coffee, sawdust, and leather—which wasn't an altogether unpleasant smell. It was rather comforting, actually. *Very shop-class-meets-coffee shop*, she thought.

Gabe hopped in the truck, soaking wet after locking up in the torrent. Water dripped off his hair and eyelashes as he brushed it off with his hands, before putting the key in the ignition. The engine roared to life, eliciting a startled cry from Lizzie, and they were on their way.

A short drive later, they were at Jovie's apartment. Gabe followed them upstairs, offering to take Lizzie's coat. The girl wandered into the living room, her mouth hanging open as if she were visiting some exotic palace. Gabe ran his hands up and down her coat, patting the pockets.

"Way to be subtle, Gabe," Jovie hissed. "What do you think she's hiding in there, an axe?"

"You can never be too careful," he whispered back, hanging the coat on a hook. "No worries. Pockets are completely empty, except for a small book."

"Really? I wonder what her plan was," Jovie replied.

The lights flicked on and off in the kitchen. Thinking they were losing power, Jovie and Gabe made their way to Lizzie. They found her standing by the dining nook, flicking the switch on and off.

She jumped when they approached. "Sorry," she mumbled, looking embarrassed. Jovie tried to ignore her strange behavior. It had been a weird night, after all.

"Right...so, are you hungry?" Jovie changed the subject. "I was thinking of getting a pizza. I'll show you where the shower is, if you want to get cleaned up while we wait."

"Pizza?" Lizzie asked.

"Yeah, what kind do you like?"

"Oh, um, I'll eat most anything," she replied. Jovie nodded and proceeded to show Lizzie around the apartment. Once Lizzie was settled in the bathroom and Jovie had pulled out some fresh clothes for her, she returned to Gabe in the kitchen and found her phone.

"Do you want to stay for dinner?" Jovie asked.

Gabe smiled, despite the strange turn the night had taken. "Yeah, I'll stick around for a bit."

∞∞∞

Lizzie stood in the bathroom, the cool tile underfoot chilling her already cold body. Jovie had graciously given her a pile of clean clothes, a towel, and showed her the bathroom. Lizzie didn't think anything could top those strange lanterns blinking on and off with the flick of a switch, or the way the café and Jovie's home seemed magically warm, despite the absence of a fire. The horseless carriage was pretty spectacular, as well. But the bathroom before her was perhaps the most wonderful thing Lizzie had ever seen on this night of encountering many wondrous things.

Back home, Lizzie had to use the outhouse to relieve herself, or a chamber pot in her room at night or when it was particularly cold. Lizzie imagined the clean, white chair that set in the corner of the bathroom was supposed to be used for that purpose. She leaned over tentatively and inspected the bowl of still water at the bottom. Curiously, she pushed down a shiny knob. A rush of water came swirling down into the bowl before being sucked down a hole at the bottom.

Lizzie jumped back at the roar of it and giggled to herself. What a clever invention! Still a bit frightened, she sat down to try it out. Marvelous!

Lizzie then turned her attention to the shiny, white bathtub. She had seen Gabe using the sink at the café, and this seemed like a similar invention. Back home, they had a large tub for bathing, but it took ages to heat water on the stove for it. And here, with the turn of a knob, hot water came bursting from the spigot. She pushed down the silver button to plug the drain, and just like that, her bath was ready. Eagerly, she slipped into the hot water, the stress of the life-changing day slowly melting away.

It was heavenly. Jovie had told her to help herself to the row of bottles lined up next to the tub, and as she soaked, Lizzie opened each one and smelled before choosing. What a strange assortment of scents! She smiled as she thought she might smell good enough to eat, once her bath was done. She shampooed her hair with a product scented as coconut milk and cleaned herself with something called cinnamon vanilla body wash.

All too soon, the water began to cool. Lizzie reluctantly pulled the plug. Standing up, she ran some fresh water to rinse off the rest of the bubbles. She noticed a smaller knob fitted into the wall. It didn't turn up or down, but when she pushed it, it gave way. There was a gurgling noise, and suddenly water was spraying directly into Lizzie's face. Coughing and sputtering, she hastily turned off the flow of water and looked up. *Ah, so that's what that spigot up there is for! That must be what Jovie meant when she said "shower." How unpleasant!* Shaking her head, Lizzie reached for her towel and stepped out.

After slipping into the dry clothes Jovie lent her and combing her hair, Lizzie wandered back out to the main room. Jovie and Gabe were seated in the main room, talking in hushed tones.

Suddenly, a bell chimed throughout the home. Jovie moved to stand, but Gabe jumped up, saying, "I'll get it!" as he rushed downstairs.

"What was that?" Lizzie asked, coming to stand next to Jovie, who pulled herself out of the chair.

"Hopefully the pizza delivery guy—I'm hungry!" Jovie walked over to the kitchen area and began pulling plates and utensils out of the cupboards.

"Can I help with anything?" Lizzie asked.

"I've got it. Would you like something to drink? I've got water, milk, sweet tea, orange juice..." Jovie pulled open a strange silver door and stuck her head inside. Lizzie leaned around to see what was inside as a blast of cool air filled the small kitchen.

Would wonders never cease? The strange cold box was filled with food and drink, kept cool simply by closing the heavy door.

Jovie turned and looked at her expectantly. Right, she was waiting for an answer. "Oh, um, orange juice, please." Lizzie wondered if it would taste as good as it sounded. Oranges were a rare treat back home. The juice sounded foreign and exciting.

Gabe returned, carrying a flat box from which

an interesting smell emanated. Lizzie felt her mouth water. She hadn't realized until now just how hungry she was. Jovie handed her the glass of juice and set two bowls on the table: one filled with purple grapes, the other with small carrots. Gabe flipped the lid open on the box for reveal a round, flat, bread-like substance with what looked like melted cheese, meat and vegetables atop it. So, this was pizza. Lizzie eagerly took the plate offered to her and sat down at the table.

Try as she might, Lizzie couldn't keep her eyes open anymore. She rolled over in the soft bed that Jovie had magically pulled from the living room sofa. Lizzie tried to commit everything from the exciting day to memory. She didn't know exactly how she'd been transported to the future or how long it would last, but she wanted to soak up every bit of it.

She thought of the false name she'd given her two rescuers. She wasn't altogether sure she wanted to share her true identity with them, or Agnes, so she couldn't use the name Cole. She'd said the first thing she could think of—her father's name, Jacob—and then added the "s" to make it sound authentic. She wondered what Lizzie Jacobs, modern woman, could be like.

Over dinner, Lizzie had peppered Jovie with questions, both out of interest and to keep the focus off herself. She could tell by the way Jovie and Gabe looked at her that they found her odd, but she wasn't too concerned about them guessing the truth. Who would believe it?

Lizzie had learned that not only had Jovie gone to college, but she now taught history classes there. How amazing that women could get an education in any chosen subject here! Lizzie wondered at the circumstances surrounded Jovie's pregnancy, though she didn't dare ask. Perhaps she was a widow?

Jovie also lived alone in her own home, as they had said goodnight to Gabe after dinner. Lizzie was still trying to figure out that relationship. Jovie and Gabe were friendly toward one another, but there wasn't that element of closeness like those who were married or courting.

Although, Lizzie noticed the way Gabe looked at Jovie when she wasn't paying attention. It was identical to the manner in which Harrison had looked at her best friend Grace when they'd begun court-ing...like she was the most beautiful and interest-ing creature he'd ever seen, and he'd take her in his arms at any moment if propriety hadn't deemed it inappropriate.

Chapter 8

Saturday morning dawned bright and clear, all evidence of the previous night's storm burned away in the brilliant sunshine. Jovie was rummaging in the kitchen, still half-asleep, when Lizzie bounded in.

"I never sleep this late!" Lizzie exclaimed. "That was the most comfortable bed I've ever slept in. Can I help you bake the bread for the day?"

Jovie jumped at Lizzie's loud voice. She had been fairly talkative last night at dinner, and whatever was left of her wariness seemed to slip away in the morning light.

"Bake bread? No, that's okay, I've already got some here." Jovie pulled out a bag of bagels from the store and popped a couple slices into the toaster. Lizzie picked up the bag, inspecting the brightly-colored label while Jovie leaned against the counter and eyed her over a steaming cup of tea.

This girl was quite a mystery. Jovie had been trying to figure her out since the previous night, but an answer escaped her.

"Tea or coffee?" Jovie offered. She had already brewed a small pot of coffee and had the warmed kettle on the stovetop.

"Coffee, please," Lizzie answered, placing the bread back onto the counter. She eagerly took the cup from Jovie.

"Sugar's right here, and milk or creamer are in the fridge," Jovie pointed. The bagels popped up and she pulled the pieces out, adding two more and placing plates, butter, and jam on the table. She had already heated some precooked bacon in the microwave and had it ready on a plate, along with two cups of yogurt.

"Have a seat," she called to Lizzie, who was sniffing the bottle of French-vanilla creamer. Lizzie grinned at her sheepishly, then poured the creamer generously into her cup.

"Help yourself," Jovie gestured to the food as Lizzie sat down across from her. "Sorry, it's nothing fancy. It's about time for me to go grocery shopping again."

"It's wonderful," Lizzie replied, spreading jam onto her bagel and taking a bite. "Thank you for taking me in last night. I'm not sure what I would have done otherwise."

"My pleasure. But, could you tell me what's going on? I'd like to help, if I can. What brought you to Redbud Grove?"

Lizzie chewed thoughtfully, swallowing slowly and sipping her coffee.

"I suppose I just needed a change. I'm all grown

up now, but as for what to do with the rest of my life... well, that remains a mystery. I just felt like I had so few options at home, and when I learned about this place, I just had to come see it for myself."

"Here, as in Redbud Grove?" Jovie asked. Lizzie nodded. Hmm, there was the university and some businesses and shops, but the town wasn't exactly a booming metropolis.

"Would you like to tell me about your family?" Jovie continued. Lizzie launched into a detailed description of her parents and younger siblings. By the time breakfast was over, Jovie had learned that Lizzie was eighteen (and breathed a sigh of relief she *was* legally an adult and not a runaway kid), that she was the oldest in a large family, and that her parents ran a farm and ranch near a very small town.

Lizzie shared that several of her friends had already married, but she couldn't see herself doing that just yet. Jovie sensed her frustration that there weren't many options for her, but why should that be? After all, it was the twenty-first century.

Then a realization hit Jovie. *What if Lizzie belongs to a religious group that avoids modern technology? That would make perfect sense. There's something very old-fashioned and homey about the way she speaks and acts. She's fascinated by the simplest things, as if she's never seen working electricity before or ridden in a car. She grew up on a farm with a large family, her friends are marrying young and she has limited choices as a young woman.* The puzzle pieces clicked into place as they cleared away the breakfast things.

Jovie's phone buzzed, and she glanced at the screen to see a text from Gabe, who had made sure to get her number last night. *Still alive?* It read. She grinned and tapped out a reply, catching Lizzie staring in wonder at the phone. Jovie felt confirmation that her theory was spot-on.

"What is that?" Lizzie asked, peering over her shoulder.

"It's a smart phone," Jovie replied. "You can send messages, make phone calls, check social media, look up anything you want to know..." she trailed off, eyeing Lizzie and gauging her reaction. Lizzie's eyes were round as saucers.

"Gabe was just checking on us. He needs me at the café in a bit. Do you want to come, too? There's no need for you to rush off, is there?" Jovie asked.

Lizzie shook her head. "No, I still want to meet Aggie. I'll come with you, if that suits you."

An hour later, the two women descended the stairs and onto the busy sidewalk. It was a beautiful Saturday. With Christmas coming soon, shoppers were bustling in and out of the boutiques around the square, arms filled with purchases.

Lizzie's eyes bulged at the cars zooming down the streets, and she grabbed Jovie's arm to steady herself. She was glad to put a name to those horseless carriages. Lizzie was picking up the new vocabulary of this world quickly. Indeed, she had barely been able to tear herself away from that talking contraption Jovie referred to as "TV" that morning, as it seemed to be a wealth of information.

What a strange time Jovie lives in. I feel rather like I'm in another world entirely, Lizzie thought, as they carefully crossed the street. This Redbud Grove didn't look anything like the town she called home. She felt quite jumpy and overwhelmed. This place was a wonder, to be sure, but she was ill at ease.

Lizzie felt as though all her senses were overstimulated. Her stomach ached a little from the strange food. There were so many noises and smells, even when inside. She had woken to the roar of the thing Jovie called a heater, the hum of the machines in the kitchen, and the people and cars outside. Did they ever just stop and enjoy the quiet?

Moments later, they entered the café. Lizzie had been too traumatized last night to appreciate much about it, but as Jovie greeted Gabe and visited with him, Lizzie took in the warm atmosphere of Aggie's business. Beautiful instrumental music played, no doubt from another device similar to the TV. Lizzie found the song had a very calming effect on her after the bustle of the town square.

Delicious aromas wafted from the kitchen, and the cheery red tablecloths and decorations around the place made her feel a sudden rush of homesickness. She reached out to touch the Christmas tree in the corner. It burned with white electric lights and was decorated with beautiful red balls. But something about the scratchy burlap ornaments scattered throughout, together with the plaid ribbon winding round it, made her miss her family so much she could hardly breathe. It looked like something Avery would decorate.

Lizzie blinked back the unexpected tears. Surely, she'd be home before she knew it. She wondered if they had missed her yet, or if the magic of the journal made it so there was no time lapse between her leaving and returning.

Lizzie had noticed the sign outside advertised a café and antique shop, and she wandered to the shop portion of the place. An unusual assortment of items was arranged on rough wooden tables. Some of the things she recognized as native to her own time, and other things were unfamiliar.

Lizzie was examining a washboard similar to the one she used back home, when a shriek and a loud crash came from the kitchen area. Jovie and Gabe nearly tripped over one another rushing to see what had happened, while Lizzie trailed after them.

She carefully pushed through the swinging doors to peek into the kitchen. Various pastries were scattered about on the floor, along with two large trays. A woman stood at the sink, rinsing her hand while Gabe gently patted her back. Jovie bent to gather the baked goods that had fallen to the floor.

"I can't believe I did that. Now I'll have to start all over! What a waste," the woman said, carefully drying her hands with a towel. Lizzie could see the angry burn marks on her hand from across the room.

"Don't worry about it, mom. You're completely exhausted from being at the hospital all week and taking care of Gram. Why don't you go home and rest for a while?" Gabe suggested.

The woman—Gabe's mother, apparently—shook her head. "I've got to start over on these tarts, and then there are the scones and muffins. There's no one else to do it, with Gram down and Deb out of town."

"We can do it," Gabe piped up, while the woman eyed him dubiously. "I don't doubt your abilities, son. You're a great cook, but this is baking. Everything has to be precise and well-timed. And you're about to get the lunch rush out there, so there's no way to do it all at once."

"Jovie'll help me, right?" Gabe looked at her pleadingly.

"Uh, sure," Jovie said. She wasn't very convincing, but then again, Lizzie wasn't sure if she baked much at all.

Gabe's mother seemed to notice the young woman for the first time. "Oh, honey, I didn't even see you there. I'm making a great impression, aren't I?" The woman rushed over to Jovie. "I've heard so much about you. It's so nice to finally meet you. I'm Emily," she said, reaching out to hug Jovie. Jovie looked surprised but returned the embrace.

"It's nice to meet you, too," she replied.

Emily pulled away. "You two really think you can handle this?" Jovie glanced sheepishly at Gabe. *She's not much of a baker, then,* Lizzie thought.

"I'll do it!" Before she could stop herself, Lizzie burst through the doorway. She'd never enjoyed being idle, and baking was something she'd been doing since she was a child. She could do it in her sleep. And help her new friends out in the process.

Everyone looked up at Lizzie in surprise. "Mom, this is Lizzie Jacobs. She's..." Gabe trailed off. The name Lizzie had given them sounded foreign to her own ears.

"She's staying with me for a few days," Jovie finished Gabe's sentence. "This is right up your alley, isn't it? You did mention baking bread this morning," Jovie addressed her.

Lizzie wasn't exactly sure what Jovie meant by the odd expression, but she did know that she could do this. "I've been baking for my family almost daily since I was a young'n. I'd be happy to help!"

"Great idea!" Gabe said. He rested his hands on the older woman's shoulders. "Mom, you're stretched too thin. Go home and rest."

Emily glanced between the three of them. "Well, if you're sure. Honestly, a nap sounds heavenly right about now. I'll show you the recipes before I go, Lizzie."

The service bell rang out front, and Jovie and Gabe disappeared to handle the customers while Emily explained everything to Lizzie. The older lady put a cap over Lizzie's hair, made out of a net, and hovered while Lizzie washed her hands thoroughly according to the directions posted over the sink.

Emily then lined up several recipes and gave

quick explanations. The enormous, shiny ovens looked a bit menacing, but otherwise Lizzie felt it should be an easy task. She set to work quickly. Emily lingered for a few minutes, but soon realized Lizzie knew what she was doing.

"Hon, you're better at working that dough than me! Why am I still standing around?" Emily chuckled good-naturedly. "Thank you for rescuing me. I'll see you later." She patted Lizzie's shoulder as she said goodbye.

Emily breezed through the kitchen doors and Lizzie was alone with her baking. For the first time since she arrived, she felt at ease with what she was doing as she measured, stirred, and kneaded with the familiar rhythms.

Emily had already shown Lizzie the control panel and pre-heated the big ovens. Lizzie slid the first batch of scones into one oven, pausing to look inside and around it. How did it get so hot in the oven without a fire? It was incredible.

She set the rest of the scones on metal trays and began clearing her workspace for the next batch of pastries. Jovie and Gabe checked on her periodically, but they were busy all morning, bustling in and out of the kitchen. Jovie loaded dirty cups, bowls and plates into a dishwashing machine. Gabe worked at another table next to the stove, cutting vegetables and preparing soups for the lunch rush.

After several hours, Lizzie finally pulled the last trays from the oven. Jovie and Gabe were just getting some lunch to eat themselves, for it was now early afternoon and the café had cleared out. They surveyed the trays and platters of goodies nearly overflowing from the kitchen counters. Lizzie had wanted to show off a little and had made a few of her specialty, apple pie.

"Wow, Lizzie, this is amazing!" Jovie exclaimed.

"If Gram were here, she'd probably never let you go. Don't tell mom or Deb, but you've outdone them," Gabe said.

He ladled out the last of the loaded baked potato soup, the special of the day, into three bowls. Placing them on a tray, along with some crusty bread and butter, he motioned to the two women to follow him. They all sat together in the café, taking a much-needed break as they ate a late lunch.

Jovie stood at the window, stretching and rubbing the small of her back. She was tired and sore from being on her feet all day, but the view from her apartment was spectacular.

Darkness had fallen outside, and the square was lit up with Christmas decorations that volunteers had been assembling all day. Strands of multicolored lights wound around the barren trees, giving new life to the winter landscape. Lighted reindeer, snowmen, and swirly Christmas trees filled out the empty spaces, while strands of lights zigzagged over them. The gazebo was illuminated, with a humbly decorated tree at the center, and a nativity had been assembled next to it. An enormous Christmas tree stretched up to the sky at one end of the square, next to a huge, red sign proclaiming, "Merry Christmas." A green one on the opposite end of the square said, "Welcome to Winter Festival."

"I've never seen anything like it," Lizzie appeared next to her, mesmerized.

"It's my first Christmas here...well, the first one living here, anyway. I remember going to the festival a couple of times when I was a kid visiting my cousins."

Jovie turned away and sank into the couch, trying to arrange the pillows comfortably. Lizzie stayed at the window.

"You're not from here?" Lizzie asked.

"No, my parents traveled a lot for work, so I grew up all over the world."

"Really?" Lizzie tore herself away from the window to sit on the opposite end of the sofa, tucking her feet under her. "I've never been anywhere. Traveling sounds so exciting."

"It is. I've got great memories of some amazing places. It can be lonely as a kid, though." Jovie absentmindedly stroked her abdomen. "That's part of the reason I moved here. I want a different kind of life for my baby. One where he or she can grow up knowing neighbors and friends...being known and loved and part of a community."

"That's how I grew up. I always loved our

farm and little town. But lately, it feels so...stiflin'. I don't know," Lizzie trailed off, eyeing Jovie's rounded stomach.

Suddenly, Jovie felt a thump against the hand resting on her belly. "Oh!" she cried out in surprise. She lifted shining eyes to Lizzie. "I think I just felt the baby kick for the first time! There it goes again."

"Really?" Lizzie moved closer, her hand outstretched. "Can I feel?"

"Sure," Jovie held Lizzie's hand where she'd felt the last kick. After a moment, they felt a faint thump, and both women squealed.

"It's your juice," Lizzie said knowingly, gesturing to Jovie's drink on the end table. "Sugar always makes babies go buck wild."

Jovie laughed. "I'll bet. Have you been around a lot of babies?"

"Oh, yes, ma'am. There are all my little brothers and sisters, plus my best friend Grace's family. I don't have hardly any memories not surrounded by a passel of young'ns."

"Maybe you can teach me a thing or two," Jovie smiled. "I'm pretty clueless about all this, myself."

Lizzie worked up the courage to ask about the baby's father. She was shocked to learn Jovie was unmarried. That the man knew about the pregnancy but had left Jovie to raise the baby on her own left Lizzie disgusted. However, Jovie had seemed to make her peace with it.

The two chatted a while longer before settling in to watch a Christmas movie on TV. Jovie popped popcorn and made hot cocoa, and they camped on the couch for the rest of the evening. Jovie stretched her feet out to the new ottoman she'd purchased from a store down the street, pulling a fleece blanket up to her chin and snugging into the soft cushions.

She couldn't decide what was more fun: watching the characters on the screen or observing Lizzie's reactions to them. The girl gasped in surprise, giggled with delight, and talked to the TV as if the characters could hear her.

Jovie had whispered her suspicions about Lizzie's upbringing to Gabe while they had been working earlier in the day. He agreed that it made the most sense, and Jovie was prepared to welcome Lizzie into her home as long as she needed.

Jovie pulled her phone out to text Gabe. *Watching a movie with Lizzie. Pretty obvious it's all new to her. Her face is priceless!*

Gabe immediately sent back a smiling emoji. *Glad you're having fun. Went by to see Gram after work and she says hi.*

How's she doing? Jovie sent back.

A little better. Moving to a rehab facility Monday to start physical therapy. She's excited to be out of the hospital!

I'm glad for her, Jovie tapped out.

She'll be bossing us all around in no time, Gabe quipped. Three dots appeared as he typed something else, and Jovie glanced up to see the younger woman watching her.

"Are you talking to Gabe?" Lizzie asked.

Jovie couldn't help it; the corners of her mouth turned up of their own volition. "Yes," she said, as she read his newest message.

"Thought so." Lizzie smiled knowingly.

Jovie turned her attention back to the phone as it buzzed. "He just asked if we wanted to meet him at church tomorrow morning," Jovie continued.

Lizzie brightened. "Can we?"

Jovie chewed on her lip. She hadn't been *exactly* avoiding the little white building not far from her apartment. Her aunt and uncle had asked several times if she'd like to come with them, and Aggie probably would have, too, if she hadn't been out of commission.

Her small circle of new friends had been nothing but kind. However, Jovie wondered what the other parishioners would think of her. Jovie was used to being around diverse, open-minded people, but this was a small town with a rather conservative population. A few of the regulars at the café had already asked about her family, just as a way of making conversation, so her single status was becoming well-known.

She had gotten a few sympathetic looks and overheard some elderly ladies not-so-subtly whispering about her. She'd tried to ignore them, but it hurt. She'd had to spend a few moments in the café bathroom composing herself before she could return to work.

A part of her wondered if attending church with her increasingly obvious pregnant belly and no husband in sight would be like wearing a scarlet letter, and if she would be made to feel ashamed for being an unwed mother. Jovie wasn't proud of the circumstances surrounding the baby's conception, but she was trying her best to do right by her child now. She wished others could see that.

Lizzie was still looking at her expectantly. Her face was filled with hope. "If you really want to, Lizzie, I guess I could join you."

Chapter 9

G abe fidgeted with his watch outside the church. He had arrived early so Jovie and Lizzie wouldn't have to walk inside alone. He knew her aunt and uncle attended the same church as his family, but he wanted to be sure she felt comfortable. He also really wanted to sit next to her.

Gabe could just barely make out her apartment door across the square. An older couple stopped to speak with Gabe and ask about his Gram, and when he turned back, he saw two familiar figures on the sidewalk, striding toward the church. Jovie and Lizzie conversed as they walked, and Gabe tried not to gawk at her.

Jovie had surprised him. He found himself counting the hours not by the clock, but by how long since he had last seen her and when he would see her again. She was kind and confident, and he admired her fierce independence and determination to start a new life for herself. She was not a girl trying to find her way in the world—she was a woman who knew what she wanted. And with the way she had taken Lizzie under her wing, he knew she'd be a great mother.

In the short time he'd known her, his admiration for Jovie had quickly turned into friendship. Now, he couldn't get the woman out of his head. If he wasn't with her, he was wondering what she was doing and when he would see her next.

Not long ago, if someone had told Gabe he'd be half in love so soon after meeting a single mom-to-be, he'd say they were crazy. He'd been wary of settling down for a while. His buddy Tyler, who'd recently gotten married himself, said that was only because Gabe just hadn't met the right girl yet.

He was getting ahead of himself. Gabe didn't know if Jovie was interested in a relationship at all during such a turbulent time in her life, much less one with him. But he could be her friend, and for now, that was enough. It would have to be.

The two women noticed Gabe, crossing the remaining space to join him.

"Hi. Glad you both could make it!"

"Me, too!" Lizzie beamed while Jovie gave him a tentative smile. She hugged her coat more tightly around her.

"Let's get inside and warm up," Gabe suggested. "Maybe we can find some coffee and donuts in the foyer." He led the way, holding the door open for both of them.

As they entered the church he'd attended most of his life, Gabe wondered what kind of impression it would make on Jovie and Lizzie. He scanned the room, trying to see it through their eyes. It wasn't fancy, but he'd like to think it was warm and welcoming. Christmas wreaths hung on the beige-painted walls while speckled, industrial carpet quieted their steps.

A table was set up at one end of the foyer with large containers of coffee and hot water for the tea selection next to it. A half-empty box of donuts set next to two platters of muffins and a large stack of festive napkins. Small groups of folks chatted as music drifted in from the sanctuary.

Jovie declined the refreshments, so after Gabe and Lizzie filled their cups, he led them through the open doors to find seats. Mr. and Mrs. Dennison stood next to the doorway, shaking hands and handing out folded papers with announcements and space to take sermon notes. He quickly introduced his friends and they made their way to some empty seats about halfway to the front.

The old wooden pews, softened with faded green cushions, squeaked as they sat down. Tall, thin stained-glass windows filtered multicolored light down onto Jovie's hands. Gabe could feel the tension radiating off of her.

"Everything okay?" he whispered, leaning his head closer to hers. She gave him a small smile and nodded. Gabe wanted to take her hand, but he simply nodded and gave her what he hoped was an encouraging smile.

"I'm glad you're here," he said.

"Thanks," she replied. The music started, and everyone stood to sing.

∞∞∞

Jovie felt herself relax as she listened to the pastor speak after the song portion of the service ended. She found his deep voice had a rather calming effect on her. The sermon was centered around Mary, after the angel had visited her and told her she was to be the mother of the Messiah.

The pastor began to read aloud, "Luke chapter one, verses twenty-six to thirty-eight."

In the sixth month of Elizabeth's pregnancy, God sent the angel Gabriel to Nazareth, a town in Galilee, to a virgin pledged to be married to a man named Joseph, a descendant of David. The virgin's name was Mary. The angel went to her and said, "Greetings, you who are highly favored. The Lord is with you."

Mary was greatly troubled at his words and wondered what kind of greeting this might be. But the angel said to her, "Do not be afraid, Mary; you have found favor with God. You will conceive and give birth to a son, and you are to call him Jesus. He will be great and will be called the Son of the Most High. The Lord God will give him the throne of his father David, and he will reign over Jacob's descendants forever; his kingdom will never end."

"How will this be," Mary asked the angel, "since I am a virgin?"

The angel answered, "The Holy Spirit will come on you, and the power of the Most High will overshadow you. So the holy one to be born will be called the son of God.

Even Elizabeth your relative is going to have a child in her old age, and she who was said to be unable to conceive is in her sixth month. For no word from God will ever fail."

"I am the Lord's servant," Mary answered. "May your word to me be fulfilled." Then the angel left her.*

Jovie found his chosen passage fascinating from a historical standpoint. As the sermon went on, he delved into the customs and culture of ancient Israel. If such a fantastic story was to be believed, Mary certainly had a great amount of faith in her God when she accepted the angel's message.

As a betrothed woman, she was essentially already married to Joseph. If he thought her unfaithful, she could have faced the penalty of death by stoning. Jovie shuddered at the thought of finding herself unexpectedly pregnant and at the mercy of the men of the community in such a context.

The story continued that Joseph was also visited by an angel in a dream, who confirmed that her unborn child was the chosen Messiah and to be named Jesus. Joseph believed the angel and took Mary as his wife.

A flutter in her belly startled Jovie. The baby had been kicking regularly since that first time several days before. It was such a strange sensation, but also made Jovie feel a connection to her growing baby.

She felt a sort of empathy for Mary—not that her circumstances were quite that extreme. But feeling scared and unprepared for the new life to come —that, Jovie could understand. Mary had only been a young teenager, from a small village in Galilee. Jovie could only imagine how overwhelming her unexpected circumstances must have been.

As the pastor continued to talk, Jovie's mind wandered. Her parents had taken her to many great churches and cathedrals growing up, and she had marveled at the breathtaking artwork and architecture. Mary and Jesus had been the focal point of many paintings and sculptures, and she could understand why Mary was so revered among the religious. Jovie wasn't sure she could bring herself to believe the story, but she respected the tradition nonetheless.

She forced her attention back to the present, to the humble little church in which she now sat. The bench underneath her creaked as she shifted to a more comfortable position. For all the great works of art through the ages that depicted the ancient story, this pastor boiled it down simply to the faith of Mary and Joseph in their God. They believed his word and altered their lives drastically to follow the plan he had set for them. In time, the entire world was changed because of their actions.

As they stood for the final prayer, Jovie wondered what it would be like to have the peace of such a faith.

∞∞∞

When the service was over, several people came over to introduce themselves to the newcomers. Jovie felt self-conscious at the scrutiny of the other parishioners, but finally her aunt and uncle came over to rescue her, and they all made their way outside. Reluctantly, she turned to say goodbye to Gabe. He was taking his family lunch at the hospital, so he needed to be on his way.

"I'm really glad you decided to come." He spoke to both of them, but his eyes were on Jovie.

She smiled back and nodded. "Thanks. Me too. It was an interesting sermon."

Gabe grinned. "I'll see you soon." He tucked his hands in his pockets as he strode over to his truck.

Jovie watched his retreating back for a moment, before being dragged back to the present by Lizzie's chirping voice.

"Ready to go shopping?" the younger woman asked excitedly. They had made plans for the afternoon, and she was eager to get started. Aunt Darla and Uncle Wayne waved goodbye, and headed off to the small parking lot behind the church.

Jovie and Lizzie drove to the other side of town, near the university, to grab a quick lunch and check out a few stores at the shopping center. The downtown area had quaint boutiques, but a few larger department stores were found at the edge of town.

Lizzie was going to look for some outfits in her own size. Jovie stood a head taller than the younger woman, so her clothes were not particularly well-fitted for the petite brunette. Jovie also wanted to browse a couple of stores that carried baby essentials.

She had her list ready and had decided it was time to start buying things.

After introducing Lizzie to the wonderful world of fast-casual Japanese food, which she exclaimed over with delight, they started at the first children's store. Both women's eyes bulged as they took in the vast array of products.

Jovie took a deep breath, squared her shoulders and grabbed a shopping cart, with Lizzie trailing behind. Soon they were deep into the baby clothing section and exclaiming over all the tiny newborn clothes.

"Is this not the most adorable thing you've ever seen?" Jovie held up a fleece sleeper with green and blue stripes and tiny monster claws embroidered on the feet.

"No, this is!" Lizzie held up an infant's Christmas dress, red velvet trimmed with ivory ribbons.

"I suppose I should wait to buy many clothes until I know whether I'm having a boy or girl," Jovie said, hanging the sleeper back up and reaching for a pack of white bodysuits instead.

"Yes, but that's such a long time to wait," Lizzie replied.

"Actually, my appointment is later this week," Jovie answered. "I can't wait to start calling the baby 'he' or 'she.'"

"You mean, the doc'll be able to tell you this week?"

Jovie nodded.

"How?" Lizzie asked incredulously. "Don't you

have to wait until the baby's born?"

"I'm having an ultrasound. It's this machine that uses sound waves to make a picture," Jovie tried to explain, gesturing with her hands. Lizzie looked appalled.

"Don't worry, it sounds strange but doesn't hurt at all," Jovie laughed.

They went back to shopping, and by the time they were done, Jovie had crossed off a few items on her list, but there was so much more to be done.

One day at a time, she reminded herself. She was barely over halfway through her pregnancy, after all. She had a good start to her preparations, and lots of work ahead assembling things. She was going to need to save up for the crib and dresser she intended to buy.

"I don't see why babies need all this stuff," Lizzie remarked, as the two of them placed the purchases into the trunk of Jovie's small car. "All we had for my little sister Hannah was a cradle, a rattle, a few gowns and blankets and some nappies," she said.

"Like I said, I'm no expert," Jovie shrugged, noticing Lizzie's use of the old-fashioned word for diapers. "I don't want to over-buy, but I don't want to be unprepared, either."

"Oh, you'll be just fine. Mamas know best, that I know for certain."

Jovie smiled as they walked to the next store to find a few things for Lizzie to wear. "Thanks. Lizzie, you've talked about your stepmom a lot. Can I ask you about your own mother?"

Lizzie smiled sadly. "My mother died when I

was little. She got sick and went downhill real quick-like. Pa married Avery when I was eight, so she's been Mama ever since."

"Do you miss them?"

"Oh, yes, ever so much. I feel a little bad, leaving suddenly like I did. This was just something I had to do, though, no matter how much I miss them."

"Lizzie, you're welcome to stay as long as you like. But do you think you should call them, and let them know you're all right?"

"I can't," Lizzie sighed. "They don't have phones like you do."

Jovie though about her theory of Lizzie's past. "They don't believe in modern technology?" she asked.

Lizzie appeared thoughtful for a moment. "You could say that. I'm going to go home soon enough, though. I don't want to impose on your kindness. You've been so good to help me. Perhaps I could see Aggie this week?" she asked hopefully.

"I'm sure you could. Gabe said they're moving her to a rehab place tomorrow. Maybe once she's settled, we could both go see her."

That seemed to cheer Lizzie up, and they agreed to make it a plan.

Lizzie stood in the guest room at Jovie's apartment, admiring her new clothes. Jovie had insisted on buying a few things for her, which she promised to pay back once she received her check from Gabe.

Today she was wearing black pants and a red and black flannel tunic. The flannel reminded her of her pa, and she missed talking to him every morning. He and Lizzie were often the first to rise at home and would take their coffee together in the quiet before the ruckus of the household waking up. She could use his advice right about now.

Was her family missing her back home? Were they sick with worry and looking for her? Would there be any time lapse once she'd returned home, or would it be as if she'd never left? Lizzie had no way of knowing. She squashed down the guilt creeping in and turned back to her reflection.

At first, Lizzie had felt strange not wearing dresses, but she had to admit her ease of movement in trousers was magnificent. She only wished she could try horseback riding in her pants and boots. It must be so much easier without those cumbersome skirts. She had planned on buying some dresses on the shopping trip, but the cut and style felt far too revealing to her once she had tried them on, although Jovie had assured her they were considered quite modest.

It was Tuesday afternoon, and she was rather giddy with excitement. She had enjoyed baking sweets for the café the last two mornings, and everyone was raving about the new variety of treats. She was proud to share her skills with the customers.

However, her baking was done for the day, and she was going to visit Aggie shortly. Jovie had wanted to come but was still at the café. She planned to stay after closing to help Gabe with the fundraiser planning.

The rehab facility was only a few blocks away, and as the weather wasn't due to turn nasty until later, Lizzie had no reservations about going on her own. Gabe had given her the directions, and it should be easy enough to find. She had scarcely been alone since she'd met Jovie and was looking forward to the brisk walk.

Her stomach churned nervously. *What will it be like to finally meet Avery's friend? And should I tell her the truth of who I am?* Lizzie realized she didn't have much of a plan, but she wasn't going to back out now. She grabbed a jacket and Jovie's spare key and ran down the stairs before her courage could desert her.

Chapter 10

Lizzie breathed in the fresh, cool air as she strode quickly past Redbud Grove's business district and into a residential area. Inviting front porches, lined with shrubbery, graced the fronts of many homes. Some houses had Christmas lights hanging from them or decorations spread over the lawns. She would have to have Jovie drive her through the neighborhoods at night—after seeing the square lit up so magically, she thought she would rather like seeing these homes illuminating the winter night.

Lizzie hadn't seen much of Redbud Grove besides the downtown area and the route to the shopping center, which was in the opposite direction. She found the homes charming and cozy on this particular street. No two looked alike. She tried to decide which home she'd like to live in, given the choice—the yellow-painted cottage or the brick two-story? Lizzie didn't realize she'd stopped until a little dog barked at her from inside a fenced yard, jolting her out of the daydream.

Rounding the corner, a sign reading *St. Mary's*

Rehabilitation Facility came into view. A post office was next to it, but the remaining surroundings were residential.

Her stomach felt rather uneasy as she stepped through glass doors, which opened automatically, and into a lobby. Glancing at the paper in her hand, she asked for directions to room 207 and was pointed down the correct hallway by the receptionist.

Lizzie paused outside Aggie's room. She heard the TV playing, but no voices. It seemed Aggie was alone. Lizzie was glad. She had been hoping for a private moment with her stepmother's friend. She took a deep breath, lifted her chin, and walked through the door.

An elderly lady with short, white hair neatly curled atop her head sat in the bed. She was covered by a white blanket to the waist. Bright pink spectacles perched on her nose as she concentrated on working two knitting needles through the pile of pale green yarn in her lap. The woman looked up, surprised to see a stranger enter her room. Nevertheless, she greeted Lizzie with a friendly smile.

"Hello, dear. Can I help you?" Agnes asked.

Lizzie cleared her throat. "I hope so, ma'am. My name is Lizzie, and I'm in town visiting. We have a mutual friend, you see, and recently I've learned some things about her past. I was awful curious about where she came from, and when the opportunity came, I jumped at the chance to see this place for myself," Lizzie said. She searched for the right words to explain.

"I...I'd grown rather unsettled in my life and wanted to make a change. But in every direction I turned, I just felt trapped. I needed to escape." Tears pricked at Lizzie's eyes. Aggie's smile had faded, and she gaped at Lizzie in disbelief. Her knitting dropped to her lap, forgotten.

"What...what is the name of this mutual friend?" Agnes asked.

"Avery," Lizzie whispered, staring at the white, speckled linoleum under her feet.

Aggie gasped and was silent for a moment before speaking. "Look at me, child. Are you saying you're Lizzie Cole, Jacob's daughter?"

Lizzie raised her eyes to see Aggie's were wide with disbelief. "I am," she said. Aggie's breath caught in her throat as she spread her arms out. Lizzie approached Aggie's bedside, carefully perching next to Aggie so as to not upset her injury. But Aggie pulled her into a fierce hug. Lizzie let the tears fall then, spilling out her worries until they were all but forgotten in Aggie's grandmotherly embrace

Aggie dried her eyes with a tissue. Her unexpected visitor had left just moments before, and she was still trying to process all that had happened. She had accepted that she'd never see Avery again, and had been happy that they were able to stay in contact.

However, Aggie had never dreamed that the time-travel could work in the opposite direction. But she could hardly argue with Lizzie sitting right in front of her, flesh and blood. Aggie had seen some unbelievable things in her life and had long ago stopped questioning the mysterious ways of God. Still, this shook even her.

Poor Lizzie had spilled the whole story about what was going on in her life, her restlessness and lack of choices with regard to her future and the unwanted advances from that young man. She confessed to reading the journal and the letters between Avery and Aggie, to putting all the pieces together and actively trying to come to the future.

Oh, what a pickle they were in now. Aggie cleaned her glasses with such intensity she was afraid she might snap them in two. She didn't know a lot about time-travel, but even she could figure out that someone visiting the future—one in which her descendants were living—might cause a problem.

She wished she could speak to Gabriel about this. His love for all things science fiction could perhaps shed some light on their predicament. But she couldn't risk telling another person.

Agnes had been gently understanding of Lizzie's emotional turmoil. However, she'd urged Lizzie, in no uncertain terms, that she must return to her own time. Lord only knew what would happen if she didn't. Lizzie had assured her that she planned to go back, but she remained vague about the when. Aggie gathered that she had gotten a taste of independence and rather liked it. She wagered Lizzie was reluctant to return to a time in which she couldn't see a place for herself.

Aggie had done her best to encourage the young girl that she did indeed have a purpose, without revealing too much about the past, or Lizzie's future. Just thinking about the conundrum had Aggie's head spinning, and she shut her eyes against the tumult. "With God, all things are possible," she said to herself.

Lord, please give me wisdom in this situation, Aggie prayed silently. *I thought it strange that you saw fit to send Avery to another time entirely, but I know your hand directed her steps and I'll not question it. But surely Lizzie must return to her own time, and soon. Are they missing her already? How much time do we have until her decisions start having consequences in our present?*

No answers came, but Aggie continued to pray for the Lord to show her what to do, and for Lizzie to find peace about returning home. Aggie picked up her phone from the rollaway table next to the bed, just as a nurse entered to take her to therapy. Aggie typed out as fast as her old bones would allow. *Gabriel, call me as soon as you can. Need a favor. Love, G.* She hit send and let the nurse help her from the bed.

Jovie put the last of the plates and cups in the dishwasher, turning on the massive machine and drying her hands with a towel. Gabe was out front cleaning the counters, and that would conclude their closing up duties.

Jovie made her way through the swinging doors and flopped into the nearest chair, leaning back and rubbing her hands over her growing belly. Her skin felt dry and itchy and she wondered how it could continue to stretch for several more months. She should probably try out that special lotion that Aunt Darla had given her last week.

Jovie glanced out the large windows. It was already dark outside, but the streetlights were on and the square was abuzz with activity. The Winter Festival started the next day, and everyone was scrambling to finish setting up booths and decorations.

"Jovie," Gabe called, tossing his towel into the basket to be washed. "Why don't you head home and rest? I can finish up things here."

"No, I'm okay. I said I'd help with the Gala planning, so here I am." Gabe had taken on so much of the responsibility at the café since his Gram's fall. She noticed the dark circles under his eyes from opening the café each morning and staying all day until closing. Jovie wanted to help as much as she could.

Jovie sat up straighter in an attempt to convince him that she wasn't going to fall asleep at any moment. She'd been up late the previous night entering in her final grades for the semester, and it was catching up to her.

"Where do you want to start?" Jovie continued. Gabe placed a thick binder on the table and sat next to her. Jovie recognized Aggie's neat cursive handwriting as he flipped it open.

"We have a week and a half until the Gala. Tickets are already sold out and Gram has everything lined up for the silent auction, which will account for a good chunk of the profit. There's a storeroom in the back of the museum where she's got all the items for the auction. I just need to check and see what's been donated and what we're still waiting on to be delivered.

"There will also be a buffet included in the price of the ticket. I need to finalize a menu, so I can get the food ordered in time, and then I feel like we need a little something for entertainment. Gram had kicked around a few ideas, but nothing nailed down for sure. And then there's the pledge sheet to simply become a museum sponsor, so that part's easy."

Jovie nodded, and they made their way over to the museum to check out the inventory first. The museum had temporarily closed until Aggie could return to work, so nothing had been done to organize any incoming inventory. The storage room was filled with treasures, although it was a disorganized mess, and Jovie exclaimed over each piece. Some of the things were donated for the auction, while others were new items that needed organized and put out on the floor of the museum.

Gabe pointed to an upholstered office chair with an ottoman as he handed her the binder. "Here, why don't you put your feet up? If you'll just read through the items, I'll find them, and they can be crossed off the list one by one."

Jovie sat down with a sigh and glanced at the itemized list. The donations ranged from antique collectibles to gift baskets and certificates donated from local businesses. She began to read off each item, and Gabe retrieved them in turn and placed them in a separate area.

It took a lot of digging, and more than once Jovie had to lend her expertise on what exactly he was looking for when the item was particularly old. Finally, she made her last checkmark on the list. They would need to make several calls to see when the missing items would be delivered.

Jovie took one last look around the storeroom. Most items were smaller, but along one wall stood an upright piano that looked like it belonged in an old western saloon. While Gabe reorganized a mess he'd made through the narrow walkway, she sat down at the bench in front of the piano and tentatively reached for the keys.

Jovie's mother had insisted she take piano lessons when she was younger. And what she saw as drudgery as a child became a thing of comfort as she got older. When she was feeling lonely in a new place, she often unwound her frustrations at the keyboard that had always made the move with them. It had become a sort of therapy for her, calming her anxious heart in unfamiliar surroundings. But as she didn't own a piano now, it had been years since she'd played.

Jovie tentatively tested out a few notes, wondering if her fingers would remember their places. To her surprise, someone had tuned the old piano. Reading music had never come easy to her, much to her teachers' chagrin. She often memorized the songs rather than read music from a book, and she reached back into the corners of her mind to recall the old melodies.

Jovie found herself gently playing "O Holy Night," one of the many Christmas hymns she'd learned. The music filled the small room, and Jovie felt her eyes well up as the song soothed her. The lyrics played over in her head.

A thrill of hope, the weary world rejoices for yonder breaks a new and glorious morn...

As she finished, Jovie heard a soft, slow clap behind her. She turned to see Gabe beaming at her. "That was beautiful, Jovie. I didn't know you played," he said.

"I haven't for a long time. I guess I didn't realize how much I missed it," she replied, wiping at her eyes. The strangest things made her cry lately, and she wasn't altogether sure she liked her hormones and the emotional fragility that seemed to come with them.

Gabe sat down next to her, the bench creaking. "You shouldn't stop." He absently tapped a few keys, and then started the right-hand side of the duet *Heart and Soul.* Jovie smiled.

"This is the only song I know," he laughed. "My sister taught it to me." Jovie waited for the beginning to come back around and began to play the lively left-handed portion. She arched an eyebrow at him and picked up the pace, and he matched her note for note.

It wasn't long until he couldn't keep up and his fingers stumbled over the keys, hitting all the wrong ones. Jovie laughed and hit a few sour notes herself, and they ended the song with an off-key flourish.

Gabe stood and bowed to her. "I surrender, worthy opponent." She smiled and let him pull her to her feet, then replaced the lid over the old keys.

"Should we get back to work?" Jovie asked.

"I suppose. The hard part's over, anyway." Gabe picked up his phone from a small table, glancing at the screen.

"Oh, Gram texted me earlier. I must have missed it. She wants me to call her."

Gabe motioned for Jovie to follow him as he dialed his grandma. They left the back room and wound through the museum. She caught snippets of their conversation but was more interested in observing the museum artifacts. When Gabe stopped suddenly in front of her, she bumped into him.

"Oh, sorry," they both whispered at the same time.

"Uh, sure, Gram," Gabe continued. "I'm at the museum and can check it right now, if that would make you feel better." He skirted around Jovie and bent down in front of Kathleen's display, lifting the quilt from the trunk and feeling around the bottom of it. Jovie looked at him curiously, and he met her eyes, shrugging as if he was baffled too. Jovie gasped with delight when she saw him remove the trapdoor. He felt around but came up empty-handed.

"No, there's nothing there, Gram. Yes, I'm sure.

Okay. You get some rest, all right? I'll talk to you to-morrow. Love you too. Bye."

Gabe ended the call. "Well, that was weird."

"What was that all about?" Jovie asked.

"I'm not sure. I didn't know there was a secret compartment in that trunk, but suddenly she needed me to check it immediately. Thought there might be something in there. She must have misplaced some-thing, but she was being all cryptic. Who knows?" He shrugged. "She's a little quirky sometimes."

Jovie glanced back at the old wooden trunk as they made their way out of the museum, wondering what secrets it held. She shivered a little, rubbing her arms against the sudden chill.

They returned to the café to work on the menu. It felt warm and cozy in the familiar room, unlike the cool, mysterious atmosphere the museum had held moments ago. Jovie felt herself perking up.

On an ordinary basis, Jovie loved food. Before she'd moved, she and Max had vowed to put their fast food college days behind them and started learning to cook together. The recipes didn't always turn out as planned, but they had fun and kept trying. Even-tually, they had a handful of recipes that had con-sistently good results. But she could always think of dishes that *sounded* yummy, regardless of whether or not she was the one to cook them.

Now that Jovie was pregnant and constantly hungry, she was exceedingly full of delicious ideas for the Gala menu. Soon Gabe had filled a page with their suggestions. He laughed as she suddenly remembered how much she loved finger foods and had a short debate with herself over whether pinwheels were superior to bacon-wrapped brown sugar chicken bites.

Gabe jotted down both. "I think we've got enough options here. I'll run the list by mom. She's going to do the majority of the cooking, along with a couple friends." He tapped the pen against the page. "This list is making me hungry."

"Same," Jovie commented, standing and stretching. Her lower back felt tight and she tried to massage the kinks out.

"It's past dinnertime. You want to go grab something? We're pretty much done here. There's that Mexican place a few doors down. We could run over there."

"Oh, chips and salsa. Yes, please!" Jovie replied enthusiastically. They grabbed their coats off the hooks, locked up the place and walked briskly up the sidewalk. The temperature had dropped, and a few snow flurries blew around, though not enough to stick to the pavement.

Soon they were seated in a window booth with a large basket of chips between them and two small bowls of salsa. Jovie hadn't tried out this restaurant yet, but the delicious aromas wafting from the kitchen made her mouth water. There weren't very many other diners around the small room decorated in red, gold and brown—just a young family with two kids and an older couple.

Soon they placed their orders and the server brought their drinks. Gabe played with his straw wrapper, flattening it and winding it around his fingers.

"So, tell me, how did you come to be a history professor? I mean, is that what you've always wanted to do?"

Jovie told him of her upbringing and traveling from a young age. "I always loved to find out the history of each place. Something about walking where ancients walked and learning how they lived their lives...it just made me feel sort of connected to the great story of humanity, you know?"

"I can imagine. That's cool you've gotten to see so many places most of us have only ever read about. I've really never been anywhere, but I feel that way about old houses. My dad mostly does new builds, but every so often would take on a remodel. That's what I loved the most, taking something old and broken down and breathing new life into it...making it beautiful and functional again for a new family. So many people want to tear down and start from scratch, but it seems a shame to lose all that history. That's why I started doing what I do."

Jovie told him a little more about the places she'd lived, and about her decision to leave the city, her old job and come to Redbud Grove. She even mentioned Parker and his apathetic reaction to the news of her pregnancy, to which Gabe just shook his head.

"What a jerk. You're better off without him," he said, and Jovie nodded emphatically.

"That's what I thought. So, I just burned that bridge and came here to start over."

When Jovie changed the subject and asked about his upcoming project, Gabe excitedly told her about the complete remodel he was going to do on an old Victorian house after the new year. "It's a total mess now, but I can see their vision for it. I'm ready to get started, but the family is working on clearing everything out of it right now."

Over enchiladas and fajitas, their conversation ranged from their work to hobbies and interests. Gabe was currently talking about his science fiction addiction.

"Yes, I'm fully aware I'm a complete nerd about all this," he raised his hands in surrender. Jovie laughed, dropping her fork in the process. It clattered to the tiled floor under the booth.

"Whoops," she said, moving to slide out of her seat.

"It's okay, I'll get it," Gabe said. He hopped up and strode over to the kitchen, retrieving a new set of utensils for her. As he leaned over the booth to hand them to her, she jumped in surprise and looked down at her belly knowingly.

"You okay?" he asked, sliding in next to her.

"Yeah, totally fine. The baby's getting excited and jumping around. I'm still getting used to it. It feels really weird, but it's pretty amazing, too." Jovie held her hands against her abdomen and watched it for a moment before meeting Gabe's eyes. "Do you want to feel it?"

"Uh, is that okay with you?"

"Sure," Jovie replied, taking his hand and placing it on her belly. "Random strangers are starting to walk up to me and touch my stomach. Personal space means nothing when you're pregnant. At least I know you."

"I don't feel anything," Gabe said.

"Wait for it," Jovie held onto his warm hand and moved it slightly to the right. It pulled him a little closer to her, and she suddenly realized the intimacy of having Gabe so near. She felt her heartbeat pick up, and then the little thump of a kick.

"Whoa! I felt that. So strange," Gabe's voice was a mix of wonder and curiosity. Deep blue eyes met hers, and she was momentarily distracted by the similarity of their color to the Mediterranean Sea. Spain had been home from the time she was ten to twelve, and many happy hours had been whiled away on the beaches of Barcelona. There was nothing like those unfathomable blue waves, yet here they were, reflected in his eyes.

Jovie dragged herself back to the present and Gabe's warm touch against her abdomen. She smiled, more shyly now than her boldness at grabbing his hand, and he returned it.

"I think you're really brave, you know," he said, his voice low and soft. "This kid really lucked out in the mom department." With his free hand, he tucked a stray lock of hair behind her ear. Jovie didn't know what to say. Most of the time she felt woefully unprepared for the new life that would be her responsibility soon.

The baby rewarded them with a few more kicks

before Gabe gently took his hand back, clearing his throat and returning to his seat across from her.

They talked about lighter topics for the remainder of the meal, and soon they were bundling themselves up and heading back into the cold. Gabe offered to walk her home. The square had mostly cleared out, and they walked in silence, but not in an awkward way.

"I'd better get up there and see how Lizzie's visit was with your Gram. She was nearly beside herself with excitement this afternoon," Jovie said. "Thanks for dinner. I had fun tonight."

"Me, too. It didn't really feel like work," Gabe replied. Jovie fumbled a little with her keys in the darkness before Gabe shone the light from his phone on the door.

"Thanks," she said, opening the door.

"No problem. See you tomorrow," he replied. She returned his smile and slipped inside.

Chapter 11

Two days later, Jovie readied herself for her doctor's appointment. She was set to have an anatomy scan, at which point they would check all the baby's measurements and make sure everything was growing properly. She could also find out the baby's sex, if she wanted. She could hardly believe that by tonight, she would know whether she'd be having a little boy or girl.

Jovie had the whole day off. Emily, Gabe's mom, was filling in at the café. Aggie was tackling her physical therapy with all the gusto Jovie expected from such a spunky lady and was making good progress. She didn't need quite so much help, so Gabe's family didn't have to be with her every moment of the day.

Lizzie had gone over to the café early to help Emily with the baking but would have Friday off.

Jovie heard the doorbell and checked her reflection one more time before grabbing her purse and going downstairs. She was amazed that she grew a little bigger every day. The comfy, light blue jersey dress she'd paired with thick tights, boots and a cardigan seemed to creep up her thigh a little farther each time she wore it. She wondered how short it would be by the time she was nine months along. Perhaps she would have to wear it as a tunic shirt instead?

Aunt Darla was waiting for Jovie on the sidewalk. "I'm so excited for you, Jo," she said, as they made their way to the car and drove to Dr. Shaffer's office.

"Me, too." Jovie grinned.

After a wait that seemed to drag on and on, Jovie's name was finally called. The technician squirted cold gel onto her belly and moved her instrument on top of it. Jovie felt awestruck as the image of a baby was projected up on the screen. She hadn't had an ultrasound done since her first appointment, and although it had been very exciting to see the baby's heartbeat on the screen, the rest of the shot had been kind of a fuzzy blob. It paled in comparison to being able to make out the baby's head, tummy, arms and legs in such detail. A tiny hand seemed to wave at them.

The technician explained what they were looking at as she took measurements. Jovie could see little eyes, nose and mouth. The baby seemed fond of sucking his or her thumb while she and Darla exclaimed over how adorable it was. Finally, the technician shifted the instrument to the baby's pelvic area. Jovie squinted at the screen, immediately suspecting, but waited for the expert to confirm.

"Are we finding out the sex today?"

"Yes," she replied.

"Well, congratulations, mom. It's a boy!"

Both Aunt Darla's and Jovie's eyes shone with tears as they hugged.

I'm having a son, Jovie thought. She would have been happy either way, but now daydreams filled her mind of being a mama to a sweet, snuggly baby boy. She couldn't imagine it any differently.

∞∞∞

The bells on the café door jingled as Jovie entered with her aunt. Gabe paused at the table he was busing and waved. She looked radiant, her face lit up with excitement. He left the tub and cleaning supplies on the table and made his way over.

"Well, how did your appointment go?" Gabe asked, while Darla approached the counter to visit with Emily.

"Everything was great. We met with the doctor after the scan, and she said everything is looking normal and on track. And guess what? It's a boy!"

Unexpectedly, she threw her arms around him in a hug. "Aw, that's great, Jovie!" Gabe hugged her back. Her belly felt funny in between them, but he didn't mind holding her so close. Quite the opposite, in fact.

"I'm so excited," she gushed, pulling away. "Seeing him on the screen, I could make out his little arms and legs and face. He kept putting his thumb in his mouth; it was just the cutest thing. It's made everything seem so much more real."

"I'm happy for you," he smiled. "Are you two staying a while?"

"No, just getting a drink to go. Then I'm going to go by and finally visit your Gram. What pastries did Lizzie make today? I thought I'd bring Aggie some treats."

"She'll love that. Let me see what we have," Gabe wound his way through the tables and to the front.

"Pick several kinds," Jovie instructed, while Emily came out from behind the counter to greet Jovie.

"Darla here's already bragging about her great-nephew," Emily smiled. "Congratulations, hon."

They chatted for a few more minutes, and then gathered their drinks and the small box of treats for Aggie. Darla had to get back home to help Uncle Wayne, so they parted ways and Jovie made the short drive to the rehab facility.

∞∞∞∞

Lizzie heard the door slam and footsteps coming up the stairs that afternoon. She smiled and stirred the pot. They were going out to the Winter Festival tomorrow, but tonight they'd be having a quiet evening in, over Lizzie's homemade beef stew. She'd had it simmering all day and had made fresh rolls to go with it.

"Hey, Lizzie!" Jovie called. "What smells so good?"

"Supper," Lizzie poked her head around the corner. "It'll be done in just a few minutes."

"You didn't have to do that," Jovie smiled, curiously entering the kitchen and peeking to see what was bubbling on the stove and baking in the oven.

"Mmm, looks delicious," she continued.

"It's not much, but I wanted to do something for you, in return for all the kindness you've shown me."

Jovie poured herself a drink and sat down in the dining nook. "It's just what I need. Today was exhausting! This must have taken you all afternoon."

"Oh, I just worked on it here and there," Lizzie shrugged. They had been on opposite schedules the last few days, and Lizzie had spent time walking around town, familiarizing herself with all the businesses and neighborhoods. She'd discovered the library and spent hours browsing books and learning to operate the free computers with internet access.

The librarian had patiently explained how everything worked, and Lizzie had surprised even herself at how quickly she caught on. What a world of information there was, and all at her fingertips. She had been fairly buzzing with it when she'd returned home, but the repetitive work of kneading bread and rising dough had brought her back down to earth.

"So, tell me about your day. How was your visit to the doctor?" Lizzie asked.

Jovie excitedly shared her news, and Lizzie

squealed and hugged her. Jovie even pulled out several black-and-white pictures from the ultrasound to show Lizzie, who marveled at the technology to peek inside the womb.

"He's perfectly healthy and growing right on schedule," Jovie gushed. They chatted for a while about nursery decorations and baby names. Lizzie could see how elated her friend was, and she felt joyful for her.

Jovie also told her about taking Aggie some treats and having a nice visit with the elderly lady.

"She's working on a baby blanket for my little guy, isn't that sweet of her? It was supposed to be a surprise, but I walked in while she was knitting."

"Oh, that's nice." Lizzie turned back to her stirring. She knew Aggie was expecting her to go home as soon as possible. She'd been very firm about that. Aggie had also mentioned she was going to have the trunk checked to see whether or not there was any correspondence from Avery.

Lizzie had checked with Agnes the day after her first visit, and it seemed that her absence hadn't been noticed back home. Lizzie wasn't sure how that worked...was time just frozen until her return? She felt relieved to know her parents weren't worried about her, and it made her feel less guilty for staying a little longer.

Lizzie pulled her coat more tightly around her slight frame. Snow flurries swirled around her as she walked the last block to the public library, and she shivered against the chill. The research she'd done the day before had left her with an insatiable thirst for more. She had the entire day to herself today, and she didn't intend to waste it.

Pushing the heavy door open, the warmth and fragrance of paper and leather assailed Lizzie and she breathed in. It was a rather comforting smell.

Avery had always insisted on filling their home with as many books as possible, though they were a rare commodity on the frontier. Lizzie's brother Drew was far more inclined to share Avery's passion for reading, but just being in the library made her feel closer to her stepmother. She wondered if Avery had visited this particular one when she'd lived here.

Agnes had informed her that three years had passed in the current time since Avery had gone to the past, though it had been ten years for Lizzie. Trying to comprehend the nuances of time-travel quite frankly made Lizzie's head hurt, and she brushed away the pesky thoughts as she made her way to the computers.

On the way, she was distracted by a bright display of newly-released fiction. Just browsing the descriptions on the covers showed heroines of all sorts, such as a doctor, detective, and archaeologist. Lizzie pulled out a small notebook Jovie had lent her and added to her list. She'd already looked into the jobs of the women she'd met since her time here and had been adding to the list as she encountered new information from the library. What she planned to do with the list remained undecided.

Once she reached the computers, she quickly looked up the qualifications for each of those careers. There were opportunities for higher education and training in each of the fields, and Lizzie just shook her head. Why was everything so backward in her own time? Was this just an exercise in futility, researching for a future she could never have? *What am I even doing here?* She felt confused and wondered if she should just leave.

"Can I help you, miss?" The librarian who'd worked with her yesterday was back.

"Oh, well, I'm just tryin' to figure out what to do with my life," Lizzie blurted out, throwing her hands into the air.

"Join the club, honey," the older woman chuckled. "You're young, though. You've got lots of time to figure it out. Have you ever taken a personality or strengths test?

"No," Lizzie said slowly.

"Oh, there are so many out there. Most are simple, with multiple-choice questions to determine how you best relate to people and work. Some of them even give some good career options to match your talents. Here, let me show you." Lizzie scooted her chair aside while the lady's fingers flew over the keys as she typed in a web address.

"There. This one's free, and you can start on it right now, if you like. I think it takes about 20 minutes."

"Thank you! I'll start right away," Lizzie replied. *What a brilliant idea! That's what I need, some direction, instead of flapping about the place with a thousand options.*

After an interesting series of questions, Lizzie selected the button which said, "view results." She eagerly read through the description, outlining her strengths, weaknesses, and how she related to others in relationships and the workplace.

Lizzie felt astonished at how accurate the test was at pinpointing her personality. She was an extrovert, and according to the test, she'd work best in a career in which she could help other people. Lizzie ran through a short list of suggestions: teacher, advisor, advertising consultant, sales representatives, social worker, and religious leader.

She had a lot to think about.

Jovie expertly swirled a crème heart on top of the latte she'd just brewed. She'd been working on different designs all week and was finally starting to be satisfied with the results. She finished the rest of the order and delivered it to the waiting couple at a window seat.

Snow had been falling steadily outside, and everything was feeling very Christmassy and cozy... at least for her. Jovie had been on barista duty all day, with Gabe's mom Emily working in the kitchen.

Poor Gabe was out canvassing the downtown businesses with fliers. After hearing Jovie play the piano, he'd had the idea to hold a talent competition as entertainment for the Gala and additional source of funds, since each entrant would pay a fee to be in the competition. He'd been scrambling the last few days to fill all the entrant spaces, with the fundraiser less than a week away.

Fortunately, Aggie was making excellent progress with her physical therapy and she didn't need family constantly hovering, or so she told them. There was a possibility Aggie would even be able to attend the Gala.

Emily had relieved them all by taking on some of the work for the week, and Sam, Gabe's dad, was helping clean up the museum for the event. It was a good thing, since most of Gabe's time had been taken up working on Gala planning and meeting with his Gram to discuss the progress.

Icy air swirled into the café as Gabe entered, wiping his boots on the mat and blowing into his hands to warm them. His ears were bright red from the cold, and he shook snowflakes from his hair.

"Americano?" Jovie asked him.

"You read my mind," he said.

"Coming right up."

Lizzie was a flurry of chatter and excitement that evening as she and Jovie readied themselves to go out to the Winter Festival. Jovie had gone home after work to change into warmer clothes and meet up with Lizzie.

Jovie couldn't help but smile at the younger woman's exuberance. She'd mentioned visiting the library that week, but this day had been by far her most productive. She was buzzing with the energy of learning about her strengths and potential career paths. Coupled with the fact that Jovie had brought Lizzie her first paycheck from the café, the tiny brunette was fairly floating.

The doorbell rang promptly at six o'clock. The two women layered on their hats, gloves and scarves and raced down to meet Gabe, who had promised to show them around. Jovie had walked past the festival the last few nights but had been too tired to explore it.

The streets surrounding the square had been blocked off as the festival spilled over the park grounds. Their group made the short walk across the street and into the heart of the action. It seemed that all of Redbud Grove had turned out for the first weekend night as they picked their way through the energetic crowd.

There were booths selling all sorts of handmade treats, decorations, and Christmas gifts. Each stall was strung with lights, and it was all so bright it almost hurt Jovie's eyes.

"It reminds me of the German Christmas markets in Europe," Jovie remarked to Gabe. She nearly had to yell to be heard over the din. He nodded.

"You're right. The festival was started years ago by a family of immigrants from Germany," Gabe replied. "They wanted to bring a little of their homeland with them, and it just grew and grew until it became this." He gestured all around them. "People come from all over to visit."

Jovie smiled as she took in all the light displays, which had seemed to expand each time she'd walked past the square. Christmas music played over the loudspeakers. Several kids' rides and a carousel were set up at one end of the park, and delicious smells wafted from food trucks and booths. Small campfires enclosed within stacked stones were scattered throughout the grassy spaces, with groups of people huddled around, warming themselves.

"How about some hot cocoa?" Lizzie piped up next to them.

"Good idea," Jovie nodded eagerly. "And something to eat."

"This way, ladies." Gabe wove through the crowd.

They spent the evening eating and drinking their way through the festival. There were silly carnival games that Lizzie insisted they all try. The prizes ranged from raffle tickets to a giant stuffed bear that Gabe won from scoring the most baskets at a shooting game. Jovie couldn't stop laughing at him as he lugged around the enormous bear the rest of the night.

Lizzie was adopted by a group of younger girls,

after she'd shown them how to properly lasso a fake cow at one of the games. They looked to be about eight to ten years old, and they dragged her around to several more games. She looked like she was having the time of her life. Jovie imagined she was missing her younger siblings.

Jovie bought a few special items for her family members and Max, who had promised to visit soon. Lizzie rejoined their group as Jovie was paying for her last purchase. When she noticed the group selling Christmas trees at the edge of the street, Jovie had a brilliant idea.

"You know, I haven't bought a Christmas tree yet," she started slowly. "Anyone up for a decorating party?" Jovie looked between Lizzie and Gabe eagerly.

"Oh, yes, lets!" Lizzie squealed, clapping her hands. Gabe agreed to help them pick out a tree and get it into the apartment. Jovie and Gabe walked slowly, but Lizzie ran ahead to the Christmas tree display, checking each tree carefully and shouting to the others.

Gabe laughed as she began sniffing each tree. "What are you doing?" he called.

Lizzie stopped and looked back at them. "It's not enough to *find* the prettiest. It has to *smell* the best," she answered seriously, and then was off and running again.

"She's such a kid," Jovie grinned. "In a good way, you know?"

"I know what you mean," Gabe answered, leaning into a pine and taking a deep breath. "What do you think? Does this one smell pretty enough?"

"I can smell it from here," Jovie answered, standing back and wrinkling her nose. "Pregnancy nose is real." She shook her head, and they moved on to the next tree.

After much deliberation, they finally settled on a medium-sized tree that smelled good enough for Lizzie but wasn't offensive to Jovie. She purchased a stand in which to place the tree, and one of the workers helped them carry it the short distance to her apartment.

Soon they were all standing in Jovie's living room. Gabe and Lizzie argued about the best place to put the tree while Jovie searched the closet for the small box of lights and Christmas decorations she'd collected over the past few years. When she returned, they'd agreed to put the tree in front of one of the big windows, and they all settled into unpacking the box of decorations.

Jovie turned on her favorite holiday music and began untangling the lights, while Lizzie scampered off to make popcorn to string around the tree. She'd learned to use the microwave a few days earlier and watched the brown bag of corn inflate with fascination.

They spent the rest of the evening decorating and chatting. At one point, Jovie paused, looking around the apartment that was quickly beginning to feel like home. Gabe had found a headband fashioned into reindeer antlers and a bright red nose made of foam. He'd casually put them on while Lizzie was scolding him about a wreath placement she didn't agree with. The younger girl tried to stay firm and keep a straight face, but she couldn't help bursting into giggles at how ridiculous he looked. He winked at Jovie from across the room. Her new friends had made her heart feel very full indeed.

Chapter 12

Lizzie woke up with a sore throat and runny nose on Saturday, and by Sunday she wanted nothing more than to lay in bed and rest. The day was overcast, with the threat of another snow on the horizon. Jovie was just saying her goodbyes to everyone at the church and on her way home, when Gabe stopped her.

"We've been working so hard, but there's not a whole lot to be done today. We can't do much until the deliveries arrive tomorrow. I was thinking of having a lazy afternoon, maybe do a movie marathon. Since Lizzie's out of commission, do you want to come hang out at my place?"

Jovie pondered for a moment. On one hand, she was extremely interested to see where Gabe lived. On the other hand, she wasn't exactly sure where she stood with Gabe. Yes, they were friends, but she couldn't deny the spark she felt when he was nearby. She wondered if he felt it, too. Curiosity won out, and she found herself nodding.

"Sure, that sounds fun. I should probably go

check on Lizzie first and see if she needs anything, and then I can head your way. Where do you live?" Jovie pulled up a map on her phone and tapped in the address he gave.

"I'll whip up some lunch. Do you want to meet in about half an hour?"

Jovie nodded. "See you then."

Lizzie was camped out on the couch with a box of tissues and a mug of apple cider. She was happy to be left alone to nap and watch TV. Jovie reheated some leftover soup from the café for Lizzie and found some cold medicine to help ease her congestion.

After changing into more comfortable clothes, Jovie touched up her makeup in the bathroom and smoothed her hair. The door was open to the second bedroom. She peeked inside, looking over the baby supplies she'd bought and stacked along the wall. Next to them, she noticed the giant stuffed bear Gabe had left. Jovie couldn't help the smile that tugged at the corners of her mouth.

He didn't live far away, and within minutes Jovie was driving through a neighborhood of historic homes. She pulled in the driveway of a small craftsman bungalow with green siding and sturdy brick pillars in front. Before she'd even gotten out of the car, Gabe stepped out onto the wide front porch to welcome her.

"I forgot to ask you—how do you feel about dogs?" he called. "I can easily put Cocoa in her crate, if you want."

"I love dogs," Jovie replied, her boots crunching

through the snow. She got slightly winded climbing up the steps, or maybe it was just her nerves making her breathing so erratic. "We could never have one when I was a kid. I used to pretend my cousins' dog was actually mine. Now, cats are another story. They make my allergies go crazy."

"No cats here. Come on in." Gabe grinned and held the door open for her.

Jovie stepped into the foyer, taking off her wet boots, coat and gloves. Beautiful refinished wood-work surrounded her, from the floor to the staircase and mantle.

"Gabe, this is gorgeous! Did you remodel it yourself?"

He nodded, an easy smile spreading across his face. "Yeah, this was one of my first flips. It was going to be an investment, but I liked it so much I decided to keep it, for now, anyway."

Gabe led her through the living room to the dining and kitchen area. The flooring changed from wood to tile, but the lovely woodwork extended to the kitchen cabinetry. The house was compact, but Jovie could tell he had spent a lot of time perfecting the details.

A large, chocolate Labrador emerged from the laundry room, wagging her tail in greeting. Gabe bent down to pet her head vigorously.

"Good girl. Now, sit." The dog sat obediently. "Cocoa, this is Jovie. Mind your manners and shake."

Jovie smiled as the dog raised her paw, and she shook it. "Nice to meet you, Cocoa. You're such a pretty girl," she patted her hands along the dog's back. Cocoa's tail thumped against the wall.

"Poor Cocoa's been neglected lately. She usually goes with me to work on houses, but Gram won't allow her in the café, obviously." Gabe moved to the kitchen sink, washing Cocoa's doggie kisses off his hands. Cocoa seemed content to stay by Jovie, as she stroked her soft fur.

"Just a couple more minutes on the chili," Gabe said. "Want to pick out a movie?" Jovie nodded, and they went back into the living room. After some debate, they had it narrowed down to a few choices.

"You know, I've never seen *Back to the Future*," Jovie said.

"Seriously? Okay, that settles it. You're going to get an education today, my friend," Gabe replied, queuing up the movie.

A few minutes later, they were settled on the leather sofa in front of the TV with steaming bowls of chili. Flames danced in the fireplace below the screen, chasing away the icy afternoon.

"Okay, so it's not the most revered of sci-fi films, but it's a classic nonetheless," Gabe said, pressing the play button.

Half an hour into the movie, Jovie reached for her drink and knocked the full glass into her lap. "Oh!" she exclaimed, the cold liquid soaking the bottom of her shirt and seeping through her pants. Jovie jumped up, and Cocoa attempted to lap up the water helpfully.

Gabe ran to get a towel, while Jovie blotted

her pants with a napkin. She was drenched, and her clothes stuck to her uncomfortably. The towel Gabe handed her helped, but she still felt a wet mess.

"Hang on, I've probably got something that you can wear. We can throw your clothes in the dryer."

Jovie started to protest, but he was already halfway up the stairs to his bedroom. When he returned, he tossed a tee, sweatshirt and plaid fleece pajama pants to her. "Will these work?" Gabe asked.

"I think so. Thanks," she said, taking the clothes with her to the bathroom. Within minutes she was dry and in fresh clothes. Even with her belly, they still swallowed her, but she felt comfortably warm. Gabe helpfully put her wet things in the dryer.

"Low heat," she reminded him. The last thing she needed was to shrink the few clothes that currently fit her.

They settled back onto the sofa and resumed the movie, but Jovie was distracted. Snuggling deeper into the hoodie, she breathed in and was surrounded by Gabe's familiar scent.

Jovie enjoyed the first movie, and they started the second with coffee and Christmas cookies. By the time the third rolled around, the caffeine was wearing off and Jovie felt too relaxed and cozy to stay awake any longer.

Gabe woke up just as the last movie was ending.

Jovie was slumped against his arm, which had long since gone numb. Cocoa had drifted off with her head in Jovie's lap. They were all tangled up in a big pile of bodies and blankets. Darkness had fallen outside, and the neglected fire had burned down to coals.

Gabe craned his neck to see the clock behind him. It was ten o'clock. Jovie slept peacefully against him. Carefully, he moved his arm, trying to stretch away the pins and needles, then nestled it around Jovie's shoulder. He tried not to chuckle as a cute little snore escaped her and she snuggled deeper into his chest.

Gabe felt a fierce wave of protectiveness surge through him as he studied her profile. His gaze moved to the rounded abdomen filling out his sweatshirt. It felt right to have her here with him. She was so independent and strong, but he wanted to be the one she could count on when she came to the end of herself. It wasn't like she needed him to take care of her, but he wanted to anyway. He smoothed her rumpled hair and gently kissed the top of her head.

Jovie stirred next to him. She blinked a few times, waking up slowly. Suddenly, her eyes flew open. She sat up quickly when she realized she was cuddled up with Gabe. Poor Cocoa jumped off the couch at the unexpected movement, looking around for the cause of her naptime disturbance. Jovie sat stiffly upright, her feet tucked under her. Her fingers wound nervously around the hoodie strings at her neck. Her eyes met Gabe's and her cheeks flushed an attractive shade of pink.

"Sorry," she said. "I didn't mean to fall asleep."

"I dozed off too. No worries," he smiled. "Guess you'll have to find out what happens with Doc and Clara another time." Gabe gestured to the credits flashing on the screen, without taking his eyes off her.

He pushed away the stubborn lock of hair falling over her face to reveal those beautiful hazel eyes. The firelight reflected in them and mirrored the burning Gabe felt within himself. Jovie watched him, her open expression a mixture of curiosity and intensity.

Gabe's hand lingered on her cheek, and he wondered if she felt the heat pulsing under his fingertips like he did. Her face was only inches from his, and he slowly leaned toward her, gently cupping her cheek in his hand. She moved slightly closer to him...just in time for Cocoa's earsplitting bark to shatter the moment.

They both jumped at the sudden noise. Gabe turned to see the dog staring out the front window, her body tense and alert. "Cocoa, hush!" he said sternly. "I've told you a thousand times, he's not gonna get you. And no, you can't eat him, either."

Gabe turned back to Jovie. "The owl that lives in that tree is her nemesis. Every. Single. Night." He rolled his eyes.

Jovie stood up, haphazardly folding the blanket she'd been snuggled under. "I should be going, anyway. It's late."

"Right. Oh, I'll get your clothes." Gabe nearly ran from the room. He returned a moment later, her clothes folded and placed in a shopping bag. "You don't have to change again. You can just return those later," he motioned to the clothes she was wearing.

"Okay," Jovie shifted her weight from one foot to the other. "Well, I had fun today."

"Me too," he said, smiling at her. She gave him a little awkward wave and made her way to the front door, grabbing her purse and boots on the way. Gabe followed her, unlocking and opening the door for her.

"Drive safe," he said. It was lame, but it was all he could think of. She gave him one last smile as she stepped off the porch to her car.

Cocoa whined next to him. Gabe patted her head. "I know, girl. I miss her already too," he whispered.

∞∞∞

The day of the Gala dawned bright and clear, the snow from the weekend having left a sparkling layer of whiteness over the town. The café was closed for the day in preparation for the evening's festivities, but inside was a hive of activity. Aggie had gotten approval from her doctors to attend the Gala, and they wanted everything to be extra special for her.

Lizzie had recovered from her cold and was ready to tackle the menu Jovie and Gabe had prepared. Together, with Emily and two of her friends, they soon had all sorts of delicious aromas wafting from the kitchen.

Meanwhile, Jovie helped Gabe organize and

decorate the space. Both the museum and the café would be in use for the Gala to accommodate the large group, with the door between them open so people could easily mingle in either place. Gabe and his father had already moved the antique shop inventory to the back of the space, covered with cloths, to make room for the talent show and extra seating. A makeshift stage was set up on a platform, and he'd had the piano brought over from the storage room.

Gabe worked on setting up the sound system and glanced over at Jovie as she removed the red checkered tablecloths and replaced them with classic white ones. Even though she'd mentioned that she was getting uncomfortable, she still seemed to move with elegance. As he was thinking this, she bumped into a chair with her belly, shaking her head at herself and moving around it. Jovie glanced up and caught him watching her. Gabe awkwardly grinned and pretended to be very engrossed in the cords with which he was working.

Oh yeah, real smooth, Gabe chided himself. He alternated between being a comfortable friend around Jovie and awkward twelve-year-old boy with his first crush. *Get it together!*

Things had changed between them after their cozy afternoon together over the weekend. Whenever they spoke, there was a tension between them. Neither mentioned their near-kiss, and he knew that was the elephant in the room. With the final push happening for the Gala preparations, there hadn't been a spare moment for them to really talk, and Gabe wasn't sure if he was relieved by their busyness or not. It had certainly made for a long few days.

Gabe had come to the realization that wanted more than friendship with Jovie. He hadn't been looking for a partner when she walked into his life just a few weeks before. In fact, he hadn't bothered dating much in the past few years, choosing to throw himself into running his business. But that hadn't prevented Jovie from coming along and sweeping him right off his feet.

It felt painful to be patient, but he knew it would be wise to give her time. She seemed to be unsettled spiritually, not to mention was on the brink of a major life change. She might not even want to start a relationship, but Gabe intended to find out her feelings about him soon. Then she could set the pace with whatever she was comfortable.

Regardless of how she felt, he hoped he could show her that he was someone on whom she could depend. He wanted to be sure she understood that wouldn't change, whether they were just friends, or something more.

Surprisingly, the fact that she was expecting a baby in a few months didn't bother him in the least. In fact, he found himself excited and looking forward to meeting the little guy each time Jovie talked about him.

Gabe could see himself being a family man. An image flashed in his mind of he and Jovie at a park, pushing a giggling baby in a swing. He imagined the pride that would be in her eyes, and it reflected in his.

"Uh, Gabe?" Jovie's voice broke into his thoughts. Man, he had it bad. He looked up to see her staring at him questioningly.

"Yeah?" he asked, trying to rearrange his features into something resembling normal, not weirdo daydreaming about the woman before him.

"Do you know where the rest of the candles are?"

"Sure, I think they're over here." He gestured for her to follow, forcing his mind back to the task at hand.

∞∞∞∞

Jovie studied her reflection in the mirror. The baby kicked, as if to remind her of his presence. She rubbed her abdomen affectionately.

"What do you think, little guy? Does mommy look all right? You should always tell your mother she looks pretty, you know," she instructed.

Jovie ran her hands over the gold-embroidered bodice of her dress and smoothed imaginary wrinkles from the flowing cream skirt. She tied the satin, empire-waisted ribbon and hoped the short dress looked all right for the occasion. She'd be helping out to make sure things went smoothly, but for the most part, the work was done, and they'd get to enjoy the party.

Of course, Jovie was feeling a little nervous about playing the piano in front of everyone, but she'd practiced earlier in the afternoon and was confident in her song selection. She had chosen a familiar tune and had only needed to polish her performance.

Jovie padded over to her closet and looked at her shoe choices. Heels felt too precarious lately, so she chose a pair of gold flats that had sparkly detailing on the toes. Bending over, she struggled to get them on her feet. How was she already so big that it was a feat to put on shoes? Huffing, she straightened and surveyed herself in the mirror once again.

"You look lovely," Lizzie said, leaning against the doorway.

"Thanks. You too," she replied. Lizzie wore simple black pants and a cream button-up shirt with a cute rounded collar. Her brown hair was pulled back in a bun, and Jovie had helped her apply a little makeup to highlight her golden-brown eyes. It made her look more like a young adult than a teenager.

Unlike Jovie, Lizzie would be working in the kitchen, keeping the food piping hot and the serving trays filled. She hadn't slowed down all day as they worked at the café. Lizzie didn't seem to mind, and Jovie wished she had her boundless energy. If they hadn't worked so hard to put on the Gala, she'd be tempted to slip into her sweats and lie on the couch all evening.

Moments later, Jovie locked up and they headed over to the café together. The festival in the square was in full swing, and the tantalizing smells made Jovie's stomach grumble. She tried to ignore it, as they arrived at the café early in order to make last-minute preparations.

Jovie had to admit they'd done an excellent job. The lighting was softened to add an air of elegance, with white twinkle lights shining overhead. Thick green garland framed the windows, and scarlet runners contrasted with the cream tablecloths. Each table held a simple white candle encircled with greenery. Several more Christmas trees had been brought in and decorated simply with white lights and red ribbon.

Emily and Sam called hello as they organized trays of food at the buffet area. Little silver pots with blue flames were set underneath each tray to keep the food hot. Jovie resisted the urge to peek underneath the closed lids. She'd named herself official taste-tester this afternoon, and everything had been simply delicious.

"Where's Gabe?" she called to his parents.

"He went to pick up Agnes," Emily replied. "They should be here any minute."

Lizzie disappeared into the kitchen to lend a hand, while Jovie headed over to the museum to make sure everything was in order. The Gala guests would enter through the museum, and the silent auction had been arranged over there as well. The patrons were invited to explore the museum at their leisure during the Gala, and Jovie checked that each display was appropriately lit with spotlights.

Jovie adjusted and tweaked everything until she was satisfied with the results. She passed Kathleen's display and paused to admire her family's collection of antiques. Not a speck of dust coated the old trunk, as Sam had carefully cleaned everything earlier in the week. She picked up the photograph of Kathleen and studied the woman whose heirlooms were set before her.

Jovie wasn't at all surprised that she felt so at home in Redbud Grove after such a short time. After all, her family had quite a legacy here. She gingerly touched the thick family Bible that was set on a small table as she thought of Aunt Darla and Uncle Wayne. *In more ways than one, it seems.*

Away from the frenzy in the café, the museum was silent. In the quiet loneliness, Jovie's thoughts turned introspective. It was almost like being in a cemetery, and she shivered at the thought. She was surrounded by all these things that had survived time, but the people to whom they had been connected were long gone.

Is that all there is, just a brief life on earth and then it's all over, back to dust? With nothing but a few possessions to show one ever existed at all? Or is there something more out there?

Jovie had always been fascinated by other belief systems but had never really felt the need for a faith of her own. Her pregnancy had motivated her to take charge of her life and live it to the fullest, but perhaps this baby was also showing her that there was more to live for than the here and now.

Simply experiencing him growing and developing was almost enough for her to believe in the miraculous. Being a part of creating a new life was certainly the closest thing Jovie could imagine to a divine encounter.

A throat cleared behind her, and Jovie turned to see Gabe watching her from a few feet away. "Hi," he said softly, almost shyly hesitant to interrupt her solitude.

"Hi, yourself," Jovie replied. She knew he felt the mounting tension between them, but they'd been so busy she'd tried to force it to the back of her mind and focus on work. But he'd acted differently this week and she'd felt his gaze on her several times. However, he always looked away quickly when she caught his eye.

Now, she was the one staring. "You clean up nice," Jovie smiled. *Understatement of the year,* she thought. Gabe was dressed in black slacks and a crisp white shirt with a green tie. She wasn't used to his clean-shaven face or his styled hair. It made his bright blue eyes stand out all the more, and he smiled crookedly at her.

"You look beautiful," he said.

"Thanks," she said as he closed the gap between them. His tie was slightly askew, and she reached up to straighten it for him. Standing on her toes, they were nearly eye-to-eye.

"This is nice, but I think I might prefer the dancing candy cane apron," Jovie teased, and he grinned back. "Everything ready to go?"

"Ready or not, start time is in 30 minutes," he said, nervously. "Although everything seems to meet with Gram's approval, so that's one hurdle crossed."

Gabe offered his arm.

"Shall we?" Jovie felt a little flutter in her stomach as his hand brushed hers, and they walked together back to the café.

∞∞∞

Gabe and Jovie were seated at a small table at the museum entrance as guests began arriving. They welcomed everyone, took tickets, and handed out the evening's itinerary. The silent auction was the first event, and the buffet was open with appetizers and drinks available.

Aggie mingled with old and new friends, carefully navigating her way through the museum in a wheelchair. She chatted gaily with each person she met. Her spirits were high, and her heart felt full at the number of folks who'd shown up to support the Historical Society. She waved at Darla and Wayne, Jovie's aunt and uncle, as she wheeled over to her grandson.

"Gabriel, I think everyone's arrived. Would you be a dear and help me welcome everyone with that sound machine of yours?"

"Sure, Gram," he replied, standing to push her toward the café doorway. He guided her to the edge of the small platform, switched off the music, and handed her a microphone.

"You're on," he whispered. "I set it up so the people who are on the museum side can hear you, too."

"Thank you," she said, patting his cheek like she always did.

Aggie cleared her throat. "Hello everyone, and welcome to our annual Historical Society fundraiser! I'm so happy to see all of you. It wasn't long ago that I thought we might have to forego the party this year, so I'm very thankful to be here and surrounded by my dear friends and community members. I so appreciate each of you and your support of our work preserving local history.

"I wanted to take a moment and thank a few people, without whom tonight wouldn't be possible. First, my grandson Gabriel, who took over the planning of the Gala as well as running the café in my absence. He's been my right-hand man while I've been recovering, and so diligent to bring my vision to fruition.

"I'd also like to thank my new friend Jovie. Some of you may know her as Professor Campbell. She recently moved to Redbud Grove and she stepped in to help with the café and fundraiser just when we needed her." Aggie searched the crowd, her eyes alighting on Jovie standing at the back. "With our shared passion for history, my dear, you might never get rid of this old lady." Jovie returned her smile and everyone chuckled.

"And finally, thank you to the kitchen team, for baking delicious treats for the café and assisting my daughter-in-law Emily with all the wonderful food for the evening. Lizzie, Jane, and Cheryl, I can't wait to dig into this delicious meal! Thank you, Emily and Sam, for taking such good care of me and filling in all the gaps to prepare for our event tonight.

"I believe the entrees are prepared, so please help yourselves to this amazing buffet. Again, thank you all for being here, and I hope you enjoy the evening."

The crowd applauded. Aggie beamed at her friends, delighted that the night was off to a wonderful start.

∞∞∞

The fundraiser was, by all accounts, a success. Everyone couldn't stop raving about the food, and Jovie had enjoyed visiting with some of her university colleagues, a few café regulars, and meeting several new people. Gabe had introduced her to some of his family members she hadn't met yet, as well as his friend Tyler and his wife Maria. Aggie's extended family was quite large, and Jovie had a hard time keeping everyone straight as they made their introductions.

As dinner wound down and dessert was served, the talent show proved to be great entertainment that kept the mood festive and lively. Jovie was satisfied with her piano performance but felt relieved when it was over. Her nervousness had made her stomach queasy. Luckily, she was one of the first entrants, so she could relax and enjoy the rest of the party once she was done. She took her seat next to

Gabe, wiping her clammy hands on the skirt of her dress.

"That was great," he whispered.

"Thanks," she said, stretching her fingers out. They weren't used to playing this much and felt a bit taxed after flying across the keys as she'd performed.

As expected, there were several other musical performances. Aggie surprised everyone by singing a song while Sam accompanied her on the guitar. Gabe's friends, Tyler and Maria, performed a duet. The next several musical entrants were unfamiliar to Jovie, but she enjoyed listening to them.

One person performed a brief stand-up comedy routine and had the audience roaring with laughter. Gabe's six-year-old niece, whom Jovie had met earlier in the evening, performed an adorable tap dance routine. One lady did a basket-weaving demonstration, while the man after her did celebrity impressions.

When everyone had had their fill of food and drink, the winners of the silent auction were announced one by one. To conclude the night, Gabe declared the winner of the talent competition. The comedian who'd had everyone in stitches with his jokes claimed the prize.

Aggie thanked everyone again for coming, and with that, the Gala's festivities were concluded. The crowd dispersed as people trickled out of the café and museum. Several groups lingered, hesitant to leave good company and conversation, while others pitched in with the cleanup.

Gabe had introduced Jovie to his sister, Amy,

earlier that evening. Her family had just arrived in town for Christmas. Amy jumped in to help clear the tables with Jovie, while a few other familiar faces disappeared into the back to help put the kitchen in order. She was thankful that the cleanup was going quickly, because she felt dead on her feet.

In fact, she had been feeling a little strange all evening, but had chalked it up to fatigue and anxiety over the event. She paused, wiping a thin layer of sweat from her brow. Jovie took a deep breath and shrugged it off as she gathered the table decorations and put them in their rightful boxes. Soon enough, she'd be home and in her cozy bed.

Lizzie watched from the shadowed doorway as Aggie looked around the museum to make sure it was cleared out, then rolled over to Kathleen's display. She tiptoed, following the elderly woman, and wondered what she was up to. Lizzie hadn't bothered to spend much time in the museum. After all, she was more interested in the future, not the past. She stopped short when she saw what Aggie was looking at.

It was all there: her pa's rifle, the family Bible, even Lizzie's own baby dress. Several other items from their home were carefully placed in the display, as well as the picture of her mother. And square in the middle stood the trunk, looking tired and worn, but still sturdy. Aggie was struggling to reach into the bottom from her wheelchair.

How could I be so daft? Of course, the trunk is here. Lizzie had assumed, quite carelessly, that Aggie kept the precious artifact in her home. She'd never thought to explore the museum other than a cursory glance from the doorway when Gabe and Jovie had first shown her around. This particular display wasn't visible from the café, so she hadn't noticed it before.

Lizzie cleared her throat, and the older woman jumped. "Land sakes alive, Lizzie! You're going to give me a heart attack."

"Sorry, ma'am. Are you checkin' to see if there's any news from Avery?"

"Yes. I can't quite reach the bottom of the trunk, though. Will you look?"

Lizzie obliged, reaching past the quilt into the secret compartment. Her hands came up empty. "Nothing," she replied.

Aggie let out a breath. "You know, I sent a message telling Avery you were here, just in case. I suppose hearing nothing means you're not missing in 1890...not yet, anyway. But really, you must go back to your own time, and soon."

Lizzie chewed a fingernail. "You know, I've been thinking. Why couldn't I stay here? After all, Avery went to the past and has made a life there. I could do the same. I like it here, and there's so much I could do," she said hopefully. "And I could still communicate with my family." She gestured to the trunk.

Aggie's face softened. "Avery's situation was

certainly unique, and even I don't fully understand it. Sometimes I feel like the older I get, the less I understand about the mysteriousness of God's ways. But he seems to have worked out all the details, and I trust that he knows best.

"As much as I've enjoyed having you here, getting to know you as a person and not just Avery's stepdaughter—your situation is different than hers," Aggie continued. "You understand I can't divulge any details, but you, my dear, have a life to get back to. There are people only you can touch, work only you can do. But if you don't return, there will be repercussions here…closer than you can imagine."

Lizzie felt Aggie's soft, wrinkled hand grasp hers. "Please, sweet girl. Heed my word," Aggie said. Lizzie pulled her hand away.

"No, not yet. I want to stay." Lizzie knew she was being selfish, but she wanted more time. There was so much more to see and learn about. She felt like she was finally beginning to understand herself, away from the preconceived notions of the folks who'd known her since childhood. Lizzie turned and ran from the room, with Aggie calling after her.

Jovie sat down next to Gabe on the stage where he was rolling power cords and placing them in plastic tubs. He'd loosened his tie and rolled the sleeves of his shirt up to his elbows. He looked a little more like himself, and the effect was rather disarming. Jovie swallowed, her throat suddenly dry, and managed to find her voice.

"Well, I think you've got a success on your hands."

He paused, smiling. "I know, I can't believe it went so well. I couldn't have done it without you, Jovie," Gabe said. "Did you see how happy Gram was tonight? She was practically glowing."

"She's pretty lucky to have you," Jovie nudged him with her shoulder. She felt a wave of exhaustion roll over her, and she stifled a yawn.

"Tired? It's been a long day," Gabe said, eyeing her closely.

"Yeah, for sure," Jovie replied.

"Can I take you home? I'm just about finished here."

Jovie nodded, standing and swaying a little on her feet. "Whoa," Gabe jumped up to steady her. "You all right?"

"Yeah, I'm fine. I'm just going to go to the restroom, and then I'll be ready to go." Jovie made her way to the small room at the back of the shop.

∞∞∞

A few minutes later, Gabe finished putting away the sound equipment and Jovie still hadn't returned. He thought of how tired and pale her face had looked, and he frowned. He needed to get her home.

Gabe made his way to the bathroom, weaving through the antique store furniture that had been pushed out of the way. He gently knocked on the door. "Uh, Jovie? Are you okay in there?"

He backed away as the door opened. Jovie stood before him, white as a sheet. "Gabe, something's wrong," she whispered.

Before he could ask what was happening, Jovie took a step forward and stumbled. Her eyes went vacant as she crumbled to the ground in front of him. He reached out and caught her just before she hit the floor.

"Help!" Gabe shouted, and he was vaguely aware of figures rushing toward them as he held Jovie's limp body in his arms.

Chapter 13

The ride to the hospital passed in a blur. Darla hadn't stopped Gabe when he'd jumped into the ambulance with her and stubbornly held onto Jovie's hand, willing her to wake up. The route to the emergency room only took a few minutes, but it seemed an eternity to Gabe. When they'd arrived at the hospital, Jovie was still unconscious. He wasn't allowed to go any further than the waiting room, and he watched, helplessly, as they wheeled her gurney through the double doors.

Gabe sat in an uncomfortable vinyl chair, the large clock on the wall ticking the minutes away loudly. Wayne arrived and sat next to him, saying nothing but patting his shoulder. A few minutes later, Gabe's mom and Lizzie came inside and sat down to wait for news. Emily explained that Gabe's dad had taken Aggie back to St. Mary's, amid her vehement protests.

The night seemed to stretch on and on, until Darla finally emerged through the double doors. Wayne leapt to his feet, with Gabe right behind him.

Darla held out her hands and Wayne took them.

"She's stable now," Darla said, her eyes filled with tears. Gabe felt the tension leave his body until he heard Darla's next words. "But the baby...they're not sure. They're going to have to run some tests."

Gabe's stomach lurched. "Can I see her?" he asked.

"Not right now. They'll be monitoring her all night, but they gave her something to help her sleep. She was pretty distraught when she woke up," Darla replied. "We'll know more in the morning. Lizzie, could you be a dear and get some things for Jovie from her house? I thought it might bring her some comfort to have her own toiletries and robe tomorrow."

Lizzie nodded soberly. "Of course."

"I can drive you," Gabe offered. If he couldn't see Jovie, hold her hand and reassure her that everything would be okay, then he'd rather do something useful. Besides, he really *wasn't* sure that everything would work out. He couldn't bear the thought of Jovie losing her baby.

"Just drop me at the house and take my car, hon," Emily came up behind him. In his haste, Gabe had forgotten he hadn't driven to the hospital. Lizzie nodded, and they gathered their coats and left for the parking lot.

The streets were eerily deserted as Gabe parked

in front of the apartment and followed Lizzie up the stairs. They didn't speak, each dealing with their own tumultuous thoughts. It was long after midnight, and the whole town was sleeping in blissful ignorance of the unsettling turn the night had taken.

"How can I help?" Gabe broke the silence as Lizzie headed to Jovie's room.

"Check the closet for a bag to put everything in," she called over her shoulder. He followed her into Jovie's room. The bed was still unmade, the gray and white comforter rumpled, and loose pillows were scattered to the floor. A few stray shoes and items of clothing were strewn about, as if she hadn't been able to decide what to wear to the Gala. The fundraiser seemed years ago, rather than mere hours.

Lizzie rummaged through the dresser drawers, and Gabe entered the small closet. He felt like a snoop checking all the shelves, but he quickly found a small suitcase on wheels and pulled it down. As he rolled it into the bedroom, the pajamas Lizzie was pulling out of the drawer caught on something. A small velvet box dropped to the floor and popped open.

"Oh," she sighed, picking the box up. A necklace had fallen out, and she retrieved the pewter-colored locket on a chain. All the color drained from her face as Gabe watched her with curiosity. She stared at the necklace in disbelief.

"What's the matter?" Gabe asked, closing the gap between them and examining the locket in her hands. There was a swirling filigree and rose pattern engraved on the front. Lizzie didn't respond. She seemed frozen to the spot.

"Oh, that must be the necklace Jovie got from her uncle. It's a family heirloom—belonged to her great-great-great grandmother or something like that. There was a box of old love letters, too, but maybe Gram still has those. She borrowed them to look at before her fall a few weeks ago."

Lizzie looked up at him in disbelief. Her hands shook as she opened the locket, but to their surprise, the necklace was empty.

"I thought she said it had two pictures in it," Gabe said, furrowing his brow. "Huh."

"I...I should put this back." Lizzie snapped the two halves together and carefully placed the necklace in the box and back into the drawer. She spun around on her heel and disappeared into the bathroom and began noisily unloading a drawer.

"Okay, weird," Gabe muttered to himself. The whole night had everyone acting strangely. Lizzie had neatly folded a small stack of clothing on the bed, and he quickly packed it into the suitcase. Jovie's robe was hanging on a hook over the closet door, and he stuffed that in the bag along with a pair of fuzzy slippers next to the bed. By that time, Lizzie had emerged from the bathroom with a bag of toiletries to add to the suitcase. Gabe zipped it up and rolled it out into the hallway.

Lizzie seemed nervous and jumpy, and uncharacteristically quiet. Gabe wondered if she was scared to stay alone, or simply worried about her friend and frazzled from the evening's events.

"You should try to get some sleep. I'll check in with you in the morning. Are you going to be okay here by yourself?" Gabe asked.

"Yeah, I'll be fine," Lizzie replied. "Are you going straight back to the hospital?"

Gabe nodded. "I know there's nothing I can do, but I want to be close by, just in case."

Lizzie patted his arm. "I'll be praying."

The lump in Gabe's throat was so tight he could barely swallow. "Me too, Lizzie."

∞∞∞

As soon as she locked the door behind Gabe, Lizzie flew back up the stairs and into Jovie's room. Yanking the drawer open and pulling the necklace out, she sat on the bed and stared at it. Her fingers shook as she traced them over the delicate filigree. There was no mistaking it. It was her necklace, all right.

It had been a gift for her eighteenth birthday from her father and Avery. Pa had given it to her stepmother that first Christmas they were all together, and Avery had scarcely taken it off since. When Lizzie turned eighteen, she had been surprised to unwrap the small package and see the locket. Avery had said she wanted Lizzie to always have a piece of them with her, no matter where life took her.

Why would Jovie have it, then? There was no logical explanation, unless there was more than friendship connecting them. Gabe had said it was an heirloom from her great-great-great grandmother. Were they bound by the blood of family? Was that why the two women had felt instantly close? It wasn't completely inconceivable; Jovie had mentioned that her family had lived in the area for generations. Lizzie was certain it had to be more than sheer coincidence.

Had she really been living with her great-great-great granddaughter this entire time? What kind of ramifications could that have? The realization of her own mortality slammed into her even as she thought of Jovie lying there in the hospital.

Jovie's and the baby's health were in jeopardy... was she to blame? Lizzie strode out into the hallway, reaching into her coat pocket. She'd kept the journal with her at all times, and she felt the need to read the words of her two mothers. Perhaps they could calm her racing heart. But her hands came up empty. The journal was gone.

∞∞∞

The dark town surrounding him passed in a blur as Gabe sped back to the hospital. He should be exhausted. Instead, he was wide awake, his thoughts far too troubled to sleep. He reached the hospital in record time. He grabbed his phone, but no messages flashed on the screen.

His eyes fell on something that was wedged in the gap between the passenger seat and console. He reached down and pulled out a small, well-worn leather book. It was the very same one he had seen in Lizzie's coat pocket the first night she'd arrived. It must have fallen out of her coat in their rush to get back to the apartment.

Curiously, he stacked it on top of his phone, grabbed the suitcase from the backseat, and strode back into the waiting area. It was deserted, and Gabe fought the urge to text Wayne or Darla to see if there were any updates. Visiting hours were long past, but he was willing to bet one or both of them were sleeping in uncomfortable chairs next to their niece.

Gabe settled the suitcase under one of the chairs and sat down, tapping his foot restlessly. He checked his phone again. Nothing.

Gabe picked up Lizzie's book. He wondered if it was interesting—probably too much to hope it was anything compelling enough to distract him. Flipping through the pages, he quickly realized it wasn't a book at all. It was a journal.

He started to snap it shut, knowing it would cross the line to read Lizzie's private thoughts, but then he noticed two things. First, the pages were worn and yellowed. And second, the date entered at the top of the page he was looking at was 1874.

Gabe's interest was officially piqued, and he didn't have anything else to do. He flipped to the front of the book and began reading. He wondered about Lizzie's connection to the journal as he began to read of the life of a pioneer woman named Kathleen and her husband Jacob.

He recognized those names. He was fascinated to be reading the journal of the woman whose picture was displayed in his Gram's museum, along with the artifacts from her homestead. He didn't understand why Lizzie would have had it, though.

As Gabe read on, things got weirder and the wheels of his mind began turning. Kathleen had died, and Jacob had married a woman named Avery. Avery became the stepmother of his three children, the oldest of whom was named Elizabeth. But everyone called her Lizzie.

∞∞∞

Gabe woke with a start, his neck stiff from the odd sleeping position in the waiting room chair. The journal had fallen to the floor at his feet, and he reached down to pick it up. He'd read the thing cover to cover, before nodding off from sheer exhaustion, despite his racing thoughts.

Dawn had broken outside, and the cloudy gray skies promised more snow. A few people were scattered in the waiting room now, and Gabe stood up to stretch the kinks out of his body. A couple sipped coffee across from him, and a young woman was tuned into her phone. It felt strange to see the world go on as normal, despite the fact that his had been turned upside down overnight.

But in the cold light of day, could he really believe that Lizzie was the same girl that had been written about in the journal? For it wasn't merely Kathleen's journal. Avery had written in it too, and her entries were far more cryptic than Kathleen's. It seemed ridiculous now, but he couldn't help his affinity for the unbelievable. Far-fetched as it was, everything made sense when he put all the pieces together.

The way Lizzie suddenly appeared in the alley, seeming so out of place in their time, from her reaction to technology to the manner in which she spoke. Her insistence on meeting with Aggie, her stepmother's friend. Lizzie had never referred to her by name, at least, not to him. But as he recalled the name Avery, it seemed modern for the late nineteenth century. *Didn't Gram have an assistant with the same name a few years ago?* Gabe tried to remember the young woman, but his recollection was hazy.

Gabe needed answers. Both Gram and Lizzie had a lot of explaining to do. Before he could gather his things, though, Darla strode through the doors. She came from the restricted area and looked like she'd had a restless night, confirming his guess that she'd stayed with Jovie.

She noticed him standing there and changed course to approach him. "Oh, Gabe, thank you for bringing Jovie's things. Did you just get here?"

He shook his head. "Oh honey, have you been here all night?" She pulled him into an exhausted embrace. "Jovie's awake, if you'd like to take this to her and keep her company for a few minutes. I'm just looking for coffee, and then I'll be back. She's in room 104."

"Thank you," he said, nearly running through the doors and pulling the suitcase behind him. He paused at the doorway, taking a deep breath and steadying himself. Nothing mattered right now except the woman on the other side of the door.

Gabe knocked softly, and he heard Jovie's invitation to come in.

∞∞∞

Jovie shifted in the hospital bed. Every part of her felt uncomfortable. The mattress was stiff, the IV in her hand ached, and the baby's heart monitor strapped around her belly chafed. Memories came back to her from the night before, fuzzy and unclear, but full of anxiety.

The last thing Jovie remembered before waking up at the hospital was going to the bathroom at the café. Something had felt just a little bit off all night, but she had pushed it to the back of her mind and focused on the Gala. Feelings of exhaustion had been her normal state for some time, but the nausea, lightheadedness and hot flashes were new.

She'd been splashing her face with cool water in the restroom when it dawned on her that she hadn't felt the baby move in several hours. He had been kicking her regularly, and late evening, just as Jovie was usually getting ready for bed, had become his most active time.

Jovie had felt her heart begin to race as a feeling

of dread settled over her. She tried to think rationally—she'd been moving around all evening, which had probably just lulled the baby to sleep. There was no reason to panic. But she couldn't shake the feeling that something was very, very wrong. It couldn't be explained as anything but mother's intuition, but she knew her baby's life was in jeopardy.

Though she checked herself for bleeding and discovered none, Jovie couldn't shake the feeling of doom that had settled over her. She felt as though the room were spinning around her, the whole world out of control as she tried to steady her breathing. She gripped the countertop for support and tried to quell the rising nausea. That's when Gabe had knocked, and she'd confided in him that something was wrong. She must have passed out, though, because her memory faded to black from that point.

She'd woken up at the emergency room, with Aunt Darla and a doctor attending to her. They'd started an IV, and though her blood pressure had been very low, explaining her fainting, her health seemed to be stable.

They had trouble locating the baby's heartbeat, however, and after having her switch positions and still not getting a good read, they brought in a portable ultrasound machine. What they found stumped the doctors and nurses. The fuzzy, gray image of the baby seemed to cut in and out. They'd locate him, and the screen would flicker and the baby would vanish, only to reappear a few moments later.

"There must be something wrong with the machine," the technician had mentioned, her brow furrowed. At long last, they brought in another handheld Doppler and located the baby's heartbeat, but it was weak and slow. Jovie was admitted for the night, had blood taken to run tests, and was scheduled to have a detailed ultrasound in the morning. Her anxiety had kicked into overdrive, but the doctor had given her something to help her relax. The medicine had made her sleep, but it had done nothing to chase away the nightmares.

A knock sounded at the door, bringing her back to the present. Darla had just left, and Jovie assumed it was just the nurse checking on her.

"Come in," she said, rearranging the blankets around herself. Jovie was surprised to see Gabe's face peek around the door. He looked exhausted, and Jovie noticed he still wore his rumpled dress clothes from the night before.

"Hi," he smiled tentatively. "Sorry to barge in on you, but Lizzie sent some of your stuff from home. And I wanted to check on you. Can I come in?"

Jovie nodded, and Gabe stepped closer. He sat in the chair next to the bed, scooting it closer to her and taking her hand. That one action spoke more than the words Gabe seemed to be searching for. He frowned at the IV, stroking her fingers before meeting her eyes.

"Is there anything I can do?" Gabe asked. She was surprised to see his eyes were as moist as hers. She shook her head.

"I'm really scared, Gabe." Jovie found she

couldn't speak above a whisper. "I'm having another ultrasound in an hour. They've been tracking the baby's heart all night, and it's been steady, but slower than normal. I don't know what they'll find. And he's been so still." Jovie held her belly possessively with her free hand. "There's a chance that there's some abnormality causing his heart to slow, and if that's the case, I...I could lose him." Her voice broke. "Do you think, maybe you could pray for me?"

"Of course," Gabe replied. "Right now?"

Jovie felt a little awkward, but her desperation was bigger than her pride at the moment. She nodded, and he bowed his head, asking God for strength for Jovie and the baby, for good health, for wisdom for the doctors and nurses, and for peace.

As he spoke aloud, Gabe's hand gripped hers tighter and she could feel the urgency of his prayer. And though her concern remained, she felt a sort of calmness come over her frayed nerves.

When he was done, Gabe didn't release her hand. They talked for a few more minutes as Jovie recounted her memory of the night's events. When Darla returned, Gabe stood to excuse himself.

"Thank you for bringing my suitcase, and well, for checking on me. And praying," she said, stumbling over the words.

"You're welcome." Gabe hesitated, then leaned in and kissed Jovie softly on the cheek. "I promise, I'll do everything I can to help."

Gabe had a determined glint in his eye as he said goodbye to Darla and walked out the door. Jovie's hand remained on her cheek where his lips had been moments before.

∞∞∞

Gabe drove directly to Jovie's apartment from the hospital. But when he rang the doorbell, there was no answer. It was still fairly early in the morning, so it was possible Lizzie was sleeping, but that seemed unlikely. He had a hunch she was already out. He got back in the car and drove to St. Mary's to see Gram, hoping he would find Lizzie there also. They both had some explaining to do.

∞∞∞

Lizzie's night had been anything but restful. She had tried to pray, but words seemed to fail her. She'd ended up on her knees, asking for forgiveness for taking matters into her own hands and running away from her problems.

As soon as dawn broke, she readied herself for the day and went outside. She tried to walk off her nervous energy and was pacing by the front door when the rehab center opened to visitors.

Lizzie wasn't surprised to see Aggie awake and in her rocking chair, phone in hand and tapping away. She didn't seem the type to sleep in. Lizzie cleared her throat, and Aggie looked up.

"Lizzie, dear, come in!" Aggie held her arms out, and Lizzie found herself snuggling into the older lady's soft embrace. The tears she had been holding all night spilled over, and Aggie patted her back gently.

"I was hoping you'd come see me today," she said. Lizzie pulled away, wiping at her eyes, and Aggie handed her a tissue from the box next to her. "Do you understand what's happening?"

"I think so," Lizzie replied. "I found my locket, and things started to fall into place. Is Jovie really my great-great-great granddaughter?"

"She is. Jovie and I had been learning about your family's history before my accident. If it wasn't all so impossible, she probably would have figured out the connection herself."

"So, she doesn't know?" Lizzie asked.

"No, she has no idea."

"Jovie passing out and the trouble with the baby...is it all my fault?" Lizzie whispered, guilt washing over her heavily.

"I really can't say for sure...this is unchartered territory, I'm afraid. But your continued presence here is sure to have an impact. Think about it, if you never go back to your own time, you won't meet your husband or have children, and all your descendants— Jovie and the baby included—would never be born."

The weight of the realization hit Lizzie like a sledgehammer and stunned her into silence. And at that moment, Gabe came charging into the room.

"Gabriel!" Aggie said in surprise.

"Good, you're both here. Now, let me just save

you some time. *I know*," he said pointedly, looking hard at Aggie. "I know about Avery going to the past from our time, and I know about you coming from the eighteen hundreds." His eyes pierced Lizzie. "If you care about Jovie at all, you've got to go back."

Lizzie held up her hand to quiet him. "Calm down, Gabe. I've already decided. I promise I'll go back to my own time. I never wanted to hurt anyone, and I'm sorry about everything. I swear, I didn't know she was my descendent, or that any of this would happen from my bein' here."

Lizzie closed the gap between herself and Gabe, touching his arm gently.

"I know you love her, and I do too. I'll go," she promised. Gabe's body sagged with relief.

"I'll go," she repeated, hoping it wasn't too late.

∞∞∞

Jovie had washed her face, brushed her teeth and hair and slipped her comfy robe on over the worn hospital gown. She felt as human as she could, under the circumstances. Darla sat quietly next to her, nervously doing a crossword puzzle. Jovie watched the monitor that tracked the baby's heart rate.

Suddenly, the little blips picked up speed. Jovie sat up straighter, getting Darla's attention and buzzing for the nurse.

"It looks like his heart rate sped up. That's good, right?" she asked hopefully, as a redhead in green scrubs strode in.

"Hmm," the nurse replied, hesitant to answer one way or the other. She lifted the paper closer to her face to examine it. "It's time for your ultrasound. Let's see if we can find out what's going on."

A few moments later, Jovie was wheeled down the hall and into a small room, identical to the one in which she'd had her anatomy scan not long ago. The tech arrived, and soon, her son's image came onto the screen.

The technician spent a lot of time essentially doing another detailed scan, but Jovie's eyes were glued to the screen. His heart was thumping with a steady, strong beat, and she noted that it was 170 beats per minute. She knew that was well within the range of normal, and she allowed herself to hope that he would be okay.

The wait after the ultrasound was agonizing, but eventually Dr. Shaffer herself appeared in her room. Jovie had only seen the on-call doctor the previous night, and it was a relief to see the friendly face of her own OB.

"You've had quite a night," Dr. Schaffer said, taking the empty chair next to Jovie and examining her chart.

"I'll get right to the point," she continued. "I didn't note any abnormalities. As far as I can tell, you're both in good health. Sometimes these things happen without much explanation. Your bloodwork came back fine, and baby's heart rate is looking good now. I'm going to let you go home, but you're on bedrest until I see you again next week. No working or exerting yourself, no lifting, just resting on the sofa or in bed. Got it?"

Jovie let out the breath she didn't realize she'd been holding. "I think I can handle that. Thank you," she said, as Darla grinned and squeezed her hand.

Chapter 14

Before Uncle Wayne's truck was pulled completely into the parking space, Lizzie and Gabe burst through the door and onto the sidewalk to welcome Jovie home. Darla helped her step down, and Lizzie pulled her in for a fierce hug.

"Easy," Gabe reminded from behind her, and Lizzie loosened her grip, looping her arm through Jovie's and leading her to the door.

"Welcome home." Gabe smiled at her. The tension she'd seen in his face that morning, mirroring her own, had disappeared.

Wayne had headed up the stairs with Jovie's suitcase and belongings, and Darla ushered them inside, carrying two floral bouquets that had been sent to the hospital.

As they reached the bottom of the stairs, Jovie felt herself lifted into Gabe's strong arms.

"What are you doing?" she asked, breathlessly.

"Bedrest," Gabe replied, matter-of-factly. Lizzie let out a girlish giggle, skirting around them and running up the stairs.

"I can walk up the stairs myself, Gabe." Jovie wiggled in his arms.

"Doctor's orders," he shrugged, with a mischievous grin. "Now, hold still!" His twinkling blue eyes turned sober. "I'm not going to lose you again," he said quietly, carrying her up the stairs.

"Be careful," Darla fretted behind them.

Jovie saw that Gabe and Lizzie had been busy that day. She smelled fresh bread coming from the kitchen, and a comforting, herb-like aroma of whatever was cooking on the stove. A vase of white roses with a red ribbon tied around it was set on the end table in the living room. Gabe set her down gently on the sofa, which they had made up with fluffy pillows and her favorite blanket.

"Are you hungry? Dinner's ready," Gabe said.

"Starving," Jovie replied, making a face. "Hospital food is the worst."

Darla and Wayne had chores to do at the farm before nightfall, so they said their goodbyes and left Jovie with her friends. Darla reminded them to call if they needed anything and said she would stop by the next day to check on Jovie.

Gabe produced a TV tray with a steaming bowl of chicken noodle soup and homemade hot rolls, followed by apple pie and ice cream. As the sun set and the sky turned fiery outside her large windows, Jovie snuggled up on the couch. She fell into easy conversation with her friends and marveled that a day which had started with such uncertainty had ended so perfectly.

∞∞∞

The next day, Jovie sat in the same place on the couch. Lizzie paced the wood floor in front of her, while Gabe calmly held her hand as Jovie took in the unbelievable story they'd just told her. There had been some disagreement over whether or not to even share with her, but Lizzie had won that debate.

The baby's health had improved the moment Lizzie had promised to go home, and so long as she kept that intention, Jovie and the baby were doing just fine. The problem had arisen the day she'd been thinking of staying indefinitely. Telling Aggie as much had tipped everything over the edge.

"Can I see the locket?" Jovie found her voice. Lizzie fetched it from the bedroom and carefully placed it in Jovie's waiting hands. She backed away, settling into the armchair. Jovie traced her fingers over the rose and swirling patterns before opening the necklace. Gabe peered over her shoulder.

"Avery always kept a picture of Pa on one side and us children on the other, but they were gone when I looked," Lizzie shrugged.

Gabe and Jovie glanced at each other and back at the locket.

"No, I think everything is as it should be," Jovie replied, closing the clasp.

∞∞∞

"I swear, it was empty when Lizzie looked. No pictures at all." Gabe shook his head in disbelief when Jovie spoke with him privately about the locket. She glanced down at the open necklace again, which now again contained the picture of Frank, along with the photo of Lizzie's children.

Jovie had also called Agnes, who confirmed the fact that Lizzie and Frank's love letters were intact. It seemed that Lizzie's future was secure, and she would find her way, despite her unusual detour. And impossible as it was, Jovie somehow found herself believing the fantastic tale of her maternal ancestor.

Jovie and Lizzie spent the next few days together, getting reacquainted after learning the truth of their connection. During that time, Jovie kept the necklace hidden from the younger girl. She knew that she couldn't share information about Lizzie's future, but she had endless questions about life on the prairie in the late nineteenth-century.

Lizzie happily obliged, chattering endlessly about her family, friends, and life in Redbud Grove as she knew it. In turn, she became completely transparent about how baffling the future was to her and how she'd muddled through, unable to share with anyone her true identity.

Aunt Darla came over every day to help, but Jovie and her friends had agreed to keep the truth of Lizzie's story a secret. They figured there was no reason for the entire town to think they were crazy.

Gabe was still busy with the café, but he made time each day to visit Jovie. Aggie had been able to go home but wasn't quite ready to resume all her work duties. She begged to differ, but for the time being, Gabe continued to run the café. Thankfully, Deb was on her way home from her family reunion and would be able to spell him soon.

One afternoon, Gabe and Jovie sat together on the couch. Lizzie had gone to see Aggie, and Darla had gone home for the day.

"I brought you something," Gabe said, pulling out a gift bag from the bookstore around the corner. "I know you've been reading on the app, but I thought you might like to have your own hard copy."

Jovie reached inside the bag and pulled out a leather-bound Bible, with her name embossed on the bottom corner. She had spent a lot of time reading while on bedrest and had tentatively asked questions of Gabe and Lizzie regarding their faith. Jovie was still new to all this, but she was curious and seeking answers. After the miraculous events of the week, she could no longer deny that God had worked in extraordinary ways, and she wanted to know more about him.

"Thank you, Gabe. It's beautiful," Jovie said, running her fingers over the gold letters.

"I was thinking about what you said, about feeling a kinship with Mary. You should read this," Gabe replied, flipping to Luke chapter one and pointing out a passage entitled, "Mary's Song."

The baby chose that moment to kick, and Jovie read the words with reverence. She felt so honored to be carrying her own son—she imagined what magnificent joy Mary must have felt at bringing the savior into the world.

∞∞∞

Lizzie filled the teacups and spooned pumpkin crisp onto blue floral plates, serving both herself and Aggie. She sat next to the elderly woman, this time in Aggie's own kitchen. She was so happy to be home, and Lizzie was glad she had invited her over. She felt in need of some wisdom and guidance and could think of no one better than her stepmother's own mentor.

"My time here is coming to an end, yet I still don't know what I'm supposed to do with my life," Lizzie began. "I'm still hesitant to settle down, yet there are so few options for me."

"My dear, I can understand your frustration. I've lived a long time, and though it was different than your experience, I see similarities between my younger years and yourself. I was ready to change the world and bristled at those who tried to tell me what I could and could not do.

"The trick is to not let other's expectations become an obstacle to your influence and growth. There will always be naysayers. And though there may be more opportunities for women here, there are plenty of other complications. We were never promised it would be easy," Aggie said.

"But how do I find my purpose where there seems to be none?" Lizzie wondered.

"You just keep on seeking the Lord and see if he doesn't guide you down a path of great adventure. Don't be afraid to take a leap of faith, and know that you'll never walk alone. My dear girl, you're a born leader. Use those gifts, and don't let others tell you that you're not enough, or that you're too much. Be faithful in the small things, and perhaps you will be given bigger things. You know, it reminds me of Timothy, when Paul wrote to him *'Let no one despise you for your youth, but set the believers an example in speech, in conduct, in love, in faith, in purity.'*

"Tell me, what would you do if there was nothing to hinder you?" Aggie wondered.

"Well, I've always dreamed of faraway places. And I'd like to work with people; I've always loved meeting people, especially children. But, not as a teacher. I never was too keen on book learnin'," Lizzie said thoughtfully. The idea to work with abandoned and orphaned children sprang back into her head.

She thought of the first time she saw Lily and Matt, her adopted siblings, standing on that train platform, their stoic faces masking their need for a loving family. And baby Hannah, the lone survivor of a terrible fire. What would have become of them without compassionate folks looking out for them when their parents could not?

There was no shortage of tragedy in the world. Perhaps she could be one of the people shining a little light to those lost and broken. It wouldn't hurt to explore the idea further. In the meantime, she would continue being a faithful daughter, sister, and friend, until such a time as God opened a different door.

Aggie nodded encouragingly as they sipped their tea. "That sounds like a good start, my dear."

∞∞∞

The Winter Festival concluded every year with a candlelight service on Christmas Eve. Jovie and Lizzie walked arm-in-arm through the square to the gathered crowd. Jovie's bedrest instructions had been lifted just a few days before, following a checkup with Dr. Shaffer. She had declared Jovie and the baby to both be in great health.

All the lights in the square had been extinguished, save for the ones on the largest Christmas tree, and a quiet peace had settled over the townspeople gathered there. People conversed in hushed tones as volunteers passed out small candles.

Jovie and Lizzie joined Gabe, Emily, Sam and Aggie, who had been allowed to go home earlier in the week. The elderly woman was doing well and had mastered the use of her walker to get around. However, she had opted to take the wheelchair for the evening, due to the ice and snow covering the ground.

Cocoa sat next to Gabe obediently. As soon as

she saw Jovie, she jumped up to greet her, tugging on the leash in his hands. Jovie bent down to love on the sweet dog.

A few minutes later, Aunt Darla and Uncle Wayne joined their small circle. Suddenly, the large Christmas tree lights went off and the square was plunged into darkness. A group at the front began humming "O Holy Night," and a large candle on a stand was lit. Jovie recognized the soothing tone of the pastor as he read aloud.

"In the beginning was the Word, and the Word was with God, and the Word was God. He was in the beginning with God. All things were made through him, and without him was not any thing made that was made. In him was life, and the life was the light of men. The light shines in the darkness, and the darkness has not overcome it. John 1:1-5.

"Life can be dark at times, but this season reminds us that we have not been left alone. Jesus came as a light in the darkness, a beacon of hope in times of trouble. And as we kindle our lights from him, we chase away the darkness and fear." The pastor continued speaking as flames were lit from the single candle. Candle to candle, the fire was passed through the crowd until the whole square was illuminated again, not by flashing artificial lights, but by the soft, warm glow of fire.

"This Christmas, we wish you joy and love, hope and peace. May the light of the Christ child dwell in your hearts. Please join us in lifting our praise for him who came to be Immanuel, God with us."

Jovie felt goosebumps up and down her arms as the crowd lifted up their voices together. It had been a rare thing in her life to partake in something so holy, so beautiful, and she felt the music well up within her to join the song.

∞∞∞∞

"Are you coming, Lizzie?" Jovie called. Agnes had invited friends and family to the café after the service ended for drinks and dessert. Lizzie still held her extinguished candle in her hand. It had been a beautiful service, but suddenly she felt like a small child who'd been away from home far too long. Her time in Redbud Grove had been exciting, but she was exhausted. Lizzie longed for the safe embrace of her parents, and to be tucked into her own bed.

"No, I'm plumb wore out. I think I'll just head on home," Lizzie said.

"All right. I'll be there soon," Jovie replied. Though it was dark, the moon and stars shone down on the snow, reflecting back into Jovie's radiant face. She seemed so happy tonight. Lizzie had sensed a change in her, and though she would miss her friend dearly, she knew everything was as it should be. She also realized it was time for her to leave.

"See you later," Lizzie said. *It's better this way,* she thought. *No goodbyes.* But at the last minute, she turned and sprinted to Jovie, throwing her arms around her. "Merry Christmas, Jovie. I do love you, ya know?"

Jovie laughed, returning the embrace. "Love you too, *Grandma*," she whispered teasingly in her ear. Lizzie pulled back, playfully smacking her on the arm.

"Hey! You're seven years older than me, and don't you ever forget it."

"Whatever you say," Jovie grinned. "Even though, technically, you're a hundred and forty-six years old."

"Shhh!" Lizzie hissed, but she couldn't help the giggle that escaped.

Cocoa barked at them from across the square. "She won't leave without you," Gabe called.

"Be right there," Jovie smiled.

"You better go on," Lizzie winked. "See you."

"Bye," Jovie said, turning to catch up with the rest of the group.

Lizzie watched as Jovie reached Gabe and Cocoa. Gabe waved at Lizzie, and she waved back as Jovie bent to pat Cocoa affectionately. Gabe put his arm around her shoulder as they walked toward the café. It shone like a beacon next to the darkened square, and Lizzie heard the swell of voices as they opened the door.

Tears stung her eyes as she turned and made her way across the snow-covered square for the last time. Jovie and Gabe would be just fine, as would she. And now, Lizzie knew what she had to do.

∞∞∞

An hour later, Gabe gathered up their coats while Jovie said her goodbyes. They were stuffed full of tea and pie, and the conversation had been just as sweet as the dessert. Looking around the warm, lively café, Jovie felt a lump forming in her throat.

Sam, Emily, and Aggie sat with Gabe's sister's family around the largest table, along with his oldest brother, who'd made it home just in time for Christmas. Ellen and Marge, two café regulars, chatted with her landlord, Bud. Sadie the florist chased two small children in the open space, while Tyler and Maria conversed with another couple from church. They had been among several new friends in the community that had visited Jovie and generously brought meals while she had been on bedrest.

Though neither her parents or brother were making the trip home this Christmas, she didn't feel alone. These people who had loved her as their own since she'd moved to Redbud Grove were practically family now. Tomorrow she'd have Christmas at the farm with her aunt, uncle and cousins. And next week, Max was coming for a visit. Jovie couldn't wait to show her old friend around her new home and celebrate New Year's Eve with her.

Jovie handed Cocoa's leash to Gabe as she slipped her arms into the warm coat he held out to her. In the spirit of Christmas, Aggie had let the dog come inside, and she had lain contentedly under the tables, lapping up any stray crumbs that fell to the floor.

Gabe held the door open, and they stepped out into the night. Jovie filled her lungs with the cold winter air, a welcome change from the heat of the café, as the dark silence enveloped them. It felt peaceful, and Gabe had gone very quiet beside her. The square was deserted, and lights shone in apartment windows as the townsfolk prepared for Christmas morning. When they reached her door, he finally broke his silence. To her surprise, he reached to take her hands in his own.

"Jovie, I know we haven't known each other very long, but it's sure been a crazy few weeks. It feels like my life really only just started after I met you. I think we have something together—something special—and I need to know how you feel." He glanced down at her belly. "If this is bad timing for you, I can wait and be whatever you need me to be. But just know, I'm here, and I want you...both of you...to be mine."

Jovie felt the tangled knot of emotions inside herself begin to unravel. She had tried to resist her mounting attraction to Gabe, a part of her feeling like she was unworthy or that he would see her as broken. But as she met his eyes, she saw nothing but love and acceptance reflected in them. She could hardly resist the smile tugging at the corners of her mouth, but he dropped his gaze down to her hands. He ran his fingers over them nervously. He rambled, stumbling over himself to find the right words.

"Do you, I mean, do you think you could ever see yourself—"

"Gabe?" Jovie cut him off.

"Yeah?" He lifted his eyes to meet hers. She pulled her hand away and rested it lightly against his lips. He looked a little worried as she slowly smiled at him.

"Stop talking." She leaned in and kissed him then. He was stunned for a moment, but then he pulled her closer, gently wrapping his arms around her. Jovie's heart raced as one hand raked through her hair, cradling the back of her neck. His stubble scratched her cheeks as he deepened the kiss. She fit perfectly in his arms, and as a delicious warmth rushed through her body, she felt the baby kick mightily between them.

Jovie knew, without a doubt, this was where they belonged. Cocoa's leash fell to the ground, forgotten. Her wagging tail thumped against them as she tried to weave in and out of the couple.

Gabe broke off the kiss, pulling away to search her face. He grinned at Jovie.

"Well, yes, ma'am. I can do that." He leaned in to kiss her again, softer and more slowly this time, and Jovie felt the heat all the way to her toes.

Jovie fairly floated upstairs. She was sure she

had a ridiculous, dreamy look on her face, but she didn't care one bit.

"Lizzie, you're never going to believe—" Jovie stopped short when she reached the living room. Lizzie was nowhere in sight, and the couch wasn't made into her usual bed. "Lizzie?" she called, walking through the apartment. It was empty.

She made her way back to the living room, sinking into the couch. An envelope addressed to her lay on the end table, nestled under the bouquet of fresh flowers they'd chosen from Sadie's flower shop just the day before.

Jovie tore into the envelope. The note was short.

Dear Jovie,

Thank you for everything. I don't know what I would have done in this strange world without you. I count myself blessed to call you my friend. But the time has come for me to go. It seems I'm leaving you in good hands, and I am so happy for you.

Give that little boy of yours a giant hug and kiss from me when he arrives. Trust your instincts, because you're going to be a wonderful mother!

Perhaps we'll meet again one day. Maybe not in this life, but certainly in the next. I can't wait to catch up and tell you all about it.

Love,
Lizzie

Jovie dabbed at her eyes with a tissue. The

apartment felt rather quiet and lonely without Lizzie's chatter to fill it, but she knew Lizzie was right. It had been time for her to go. Lizzie had a life to get back to in 1890, and Jovie couldn't wait for her friend to discover all the wonderful things she would do with it.

Jovie readied herself for bed, slipping into her favorite flannel pajamas and throwing her robe on over them. She walked through her apartment, turning off all the lights before heading off to bed. But she left the Christmas tree lights in the window aglow.

Jovie looked out over the peaceful, slumbering town. She was so happy she'd taken a chance on Redbud Grove. She rested her hand over her belly as the baby kicked again.

"We're home, little one," she whispered. "And it's going to be a very merry Christmas."

Epilogue

Spring 1891

Lizzie stepped out onto the bustling train platform, strange noises, sights and smells all around her. The exhaustion from her trip was overshadowed by her excitement at finally arriving in New York City. She was sure she looked a sight, but she attempted to smooth the wrinkles of her shirtwaist and jacket, lifting her chin in determination.

Lizzie made her way out of the crowd, searching for Mr. Thomson. He was an employee of the Children's Aid Society and was to meet her and escort her to her new home.

A tall, blond man dressed a well-worn suit caught her eye. His full beard made him look rather severe. Then he smiled at two children passing by with their mother. That look, paired with his kind eyes, transformed him into someone almost boyishly charming.

"Miss Elizabeth Cole?" he inquired as he reached her, doffing his hat. She'd always gone by Lizzie, but she rather liked the sound of her full name when he said it.

"Yes. Mr. Thomson, is it?"

"Yes, miss. Frank Thomson." He shook her hand, his green eyes sparkling with warmth. She knew from her letters with Avery's contact that he had been with the Society for a couple of years and had made the trip west a few times.

"Pleased to make your acquaintance," Lizzie said.

"Same to you. We are all very glad to have you —especially the children. Tell me, do you know any good stories?" he asked, conspiratorially. "I'm under strict instructions from a young lad named Edward to ask. Apparently, he's grown rather tired of my old tales. And Rosie wants to know if you can braid hair. I can never quite reach her standards," he said, chuckling. Lizzie laughed along, imagining the large man attempting to braid a little girl's hair. She knew it had taken her own Pa ages to figure out how to do hers after her mother passed, and by that time, she had learned how to do it herself.

"You're in luck, Mr. Thomson. That's a 'yes,' on both accounts."

"Very well, then. I suppose you'll meet their approval. Now, shall we collect your luggage?" Lizzie took his offered arm as she walked toward her new life.

December 2019

Jovie woke slowly, stretching and yawning. Light filtered in through the sheer curtains on her bedroom window. She hadn't gotten enough sleep, but adequate rest was a rarity these days. Baby Griffin was seven months old now, and deep in the throes of teething. She had spent most of the night in the rocking chair, trying to comfort him. In the early morning hours, Gabe had taken the baby and insisted she go back to bed.

Jovie smiled sleepily, thinking of her new husband. They had married just a few weeks ago, on a cool, frosty evening. In a simple candlelight ceremony, they had pledged their lives to one another in front of a few family members and friends. They had tried to take things slowly but were both too eager to begin their life together to wait any longer.

Gabe's side of the bed was cold and empty, but she could hear his voice coming from the living room. Jovie threw on the fleece pajama pants he'd loaned her so long ago. She'd never given them back, and now they were her favorite. She slipped into her cozy robe and slippers, eager to see her family. A quick peek into Griffin's room showed his crib was vacant, too, and happy shrieks down the hall confirmed he was awake.

The aromas of coffee and burned toast swirled around Jovie. Burning food was so unlike Gabe, but she knew how demanding Griffin could be. Jovie paused in the doorway, watching her husband and son. They sat on a blanket next to the Christmas tree, a tall, narrow pine they'd decorated over the weekend. Most of the ornaments nearest the floor had been removed the last few days, as Jovie discovered that Griffin's newly found mobility and curiosity did not mix well with breakable decor.

But with his increasing independence also came a developing personality. He was a happy baby —when he was feeling well, that is—and full of joy and energy. Jovie never knew she could love someone so completely and without question, despite his demands on her time and energy.

And Gabe loved the both of them so well. Jovie had been concerned that she came as a package deal, but Gabe had never shown anything but kindness and love to both her and her son. He'd been with her when she gave birth to Griffin, holding her hand and whispering words of encouragement when she felt she couldn't do it anymore.

When he'd finally arrived after a very long labor, Gabe had assured her a more beautiful baby boy and mother there had never been. Griffin's biological father signed over his rights, and Gabe was already in the process of completing the adoption paperwork to make him officially his son.

Jovie listened to Griffin's squeals of delight as Gabe found the ticklish spot under his chin. Cocoa slept under the tree, her ears twitching each time Griffin cried out. Jovie watched them, savoring the moment and tucking it away it into her memory to treasure forever.

Jovie wondered how she had ever gotten so lucky. Although, perhaps it wasn't luck at all. Jovie had learned far more about God's love and guidance in the past year than she ever thought possible.

The love she shared with Gabe was real and true and good. It was not found in elaborate gestures or grand displays, no—this forever love she had been blessed with was a thousand everyday moments, knitted together from all the messy, wondrous, and even heartbreaking moments.

The past year had been full of ups and downs, joys and heartache. She thought of Griffin's birth and her wedding day, and all the moments in between. The memories flashed by like snapshots. Waking up in the hospital with Gabe holding her hand. Crying in the darkness from the impossible task of mothering a sleepless infant, and Gabe's strong arms comforting her. The two of them administering every comfort they could think of when Griffin had his first fever and Gabe holding him in the steaming bathroom when he came down with croup. Enjoying their favorite coffee and tea together in the nook on the rare mornings when the baby slept in. Holding each other's hands tightly at old Bud's funeral and sobbing together in relief after Aunt Darla's cancer scare. Gabe working on the weekends remodeling the home they bought on the edge of town, and slowly turning it into a home for the three of them. The elation she'd shared with him with the university's full-time job offer, after Professor Black made the decision to retire. Last of all, Gabe giving her an early Christmas present—the piano that now graced the far wall of the living room and filled their home with music.

The well of memories seemed never-ending, and to think Jovie had only met Gabe a little over a year ago. She couldn't wait to make him her forever.

∞∞∞

Gabe looked up from Griffin's chubby, giggling face to find Jovie watching them thoughtfully from the hallway. Her fluffy grey robe was pulled tightly around her against the morning chill and her hand rested over her heart. There were sleep creases on one side of her face where she had burrowed into her pillow and her hair, grown out since they'd first met, was pulled up into a messy bun atop her head. Even so, she smiled, and love shone through her sleepy eyes.

"Morning, beautiful," Gabe said, as she moved to join them. She kissed Griffin's rosy cheeks as he batted at her face and snuggled into Gabe's side.

"Hi, you," she whispered. "Thanks for letting me sleep."

Gabe stroked the top of her head. "You're welcome." She smelled like cinnamon and vanilla, mixed with Griffin's baby smell on her shoulder. He held her close, wishing he could freeze this moment in time. This woman brought him such love and joy, and he wanted her by his side for all the days God would give them.

All too soon, Griffin's curiosity got the better of him as he crawled—wobbled, really—toward the Christmas tree and batted at the branches. He looked back and forth between the dog and the tree, finally deciding to climb on top of Cocoa to reach the elusive branch more easily. Reluctantly, Gabe stood and pulled Jovie to her feet. She whisked Griffin away from the tree and handed him a teething toy instead.

"All right, little man," she said, pulling out his high chair. "How about some breakfast? Who wants apple-prune-butternut squash?" she asked sweetly, then turned to Gabe and made a gagging face.

Gabe chuckled and tossed the ruined toast in the trash can, starting a fresh batch and firing up the kettle. "Tea, hon?"

"Always," she said, collecting a bowl and spoon from the cabinets. He caught the belt of her robe from the back and pulled her to him.

"Hey!" Jovie protested, but Gabe turned her toward him and silenced her with a kiss. It was slow and soft, and it warmed him all over.

"You have my attention," she smiled as he pulled away.

"I love you, Jovie Taylor. From the moment you walked into Gram's café, I knew my life would never be the same." He cupped her face with his hands, searching those hazel eyes he'd come to know so well. "With all the impossible things we've been through in the last year, what amazes me the most is that you chose me."

"Well, you're not so bad. I think I'll keep you," Jovie teased. Her voice softened. "I love you too, Gabe. Always and forever." She leaned in for another kiss, but the moment was broken by Griffin's toy clattering to the floor and his impatient cry for breakfast.

Smiling and shrugging, Jovie turned her attention to their son while Gabe poured her tea. He settled down at the breakfast table with his family, hoping for a thousand more mornings such as this. They had nothing but time.

THE END.

A Note from the Author

Thank you for purchasing *A Tale of Christmas Present*! I hope you enjoyed reading it and getting into the holiday spirit. If you feel so inclined, please leave a review on Amazon or Goodreads and follow my Facebook page for news about upcoming projects!

The more I write, the more I've come to the realization that books are a lot like babies. While I was writing this, my second published book, during the past year, I wondered if I could ever love it as much as *A Tale of Christmas Past*. That book was my first baby. And just as happened with my real children, I found myself loving this story just as much as my first one.

I hope this book touched you in some way, and I'm honored that you spent your time reading it. If you are also struggling with finding purpose, I pray you will not only find your way, but also discover joy along the journey with the people you encounter and the lives you touch.

I know it's been a difficult year for some, and at times the world feels so painful and chaotic. May we all remember, at Christmastime and throughout the year, the power that we hold to spread love and kindness to our fellow humans. We can never know what small gesture can make a world of difference to someone else. May we be beacons of peace and hope in this world, chasing away the darkness.

Happy Reading,
Katelyn A. Brown